LIGHT MAGIC

RITE WORLD: FALLEN ANGEL
BOOK 2

JULIANA HAYGERT

COPYRIGHT

This book is a work of fiction. Names, characters, places, and incidents either are products of the author's imagination or are used fictitiously. Any resemblance to actual persons, living or dead, events, or locales is entirely coincidental.

Copyright © 2024 by Dark Witch Press, LLC

All rights reserved. This book or any portion thereof may not be reproduced or used in any manner whatsoever without the express written permission of the publisher except for the use of brief quotations in a book review.

Manufactured in the United States of America.

First Edition May 24

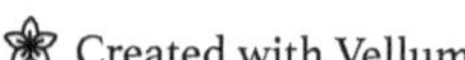
www.JulianaHaygert.com

Edited by H. Danielle Crabtree

Proofread by Kimberly Cannon

Cover design by Jes Ireland from Black Bird Book Covers

Any trademark, service marks, product names, or names featured are the property of their respective owners, and are used only for reference. There is no implied endorsement if one of these terms is used.

❀ Created with Vellum

RITE WORLD

Welcome to the RITE WORLD!

For a printable reading order, click here!

Free Novellas:
The Vampire Hunt
The Light Witch

Novellas:
The Hunter Path
The Light Calling
The Light Witch
The Wicked Alliance
The Shadow Fae
The Fae Queen

The Wild Wolf
The Vampire Princess
Snow Hunt

Rite World:
The Vampire Heir (Book 1)
The Witch Queen (Book 2)
The Immortal Vow (Book 3)
The Warlock Lord (Book 4)
The Wolf Consort (Book 5)
The Crystal Rose (Book 6)
The Wolf Forsaken (Book 7)
The Fae Bound (Book 8)
The Blood Pact (Book 9)

Rite World: Blackthorn Hunters Academy
The Demons Kiss (Book 1)
The Hunter Secret (Book 2)
The Soul Bond (Book 3)
The Shadow Trials (Book 4)
The Immortal Vow (Book 5)

Rite World: Vampire Wars
The Darkest Vampire (Book 1)
The Darkest Witch (Book 2)
The Darkest Magic (Book 3)

Rite World: Night Wolves
The Night Calling (Book 1)
The Night Burning (Book 2)
The Night Hunting (Book 3)

The Night Rising (Book 4)

Rite World: Lightgrove Witches
The Midnight Test (Book 1)
The Midnight Spell (Book 2)
The Midnight Flame (Book 3)
The Midnight Secret (Book 4)
The Midnight Hunt (Book 5)
The Midnight Wish (Book 6)

Rite World: Fallen Angel
Dark Wings (Book 1)
Light Magic (Book 2)
Fallen Demon (Book 3)
Wicked Angel (Book 4)

And more to come!

AUTHOR'S NOTE

I hope you enjoy reading *Light Magic*!

This book is set in a bigger "universe", called **Rite World**, where many of my series take place. This "universe" is still our modern world, but with a large, hidden supernatural society. Because there are many series in this same universe, there will be many cameos in my books, but don't worry. Book 1 of any new series is designed to be a good entry point into this universe. Hopefully, you'll like it a lot and will pick up the other books too! <3

If you want to see exclusive teasers, help me decide on covers, read excerpts, talk about books, etc, join my reader group on Facebook: Juliana's Club!

DISCLAIMER

Disclaimer: since this book is set in the Rite World, there are mild spoilers here and there, like most books set in this universe. However, in this one, I spoil a lot of the ending of The Night Hunting, which is book 3 in the Rite World: Night Wolves series. If you've already read that one, go ahead without fear. If you haven't, but you're on the fence, I would suggest you read that series before this one. But if you don't mind reading the spoilers, then keep reading! ;)

1

Things weren't going my way.

Several years ago, I lost my wings and my Celestial Blade. Then about seven months ago, a higher demon stole my magic.

And two weeks ago, when things seemed to finally be aligning, I was hurt again.

This one shouldn't matter.

Because I knew Levi was an evil demon from the beginning, I knew I shouldn't trust him, and yet, I lowered my guard. I let him mess with my head. I almost let him mess with my heart. And in the end, he was just using me for his own gains.

It shouldn't matter but it freaking hurt.

I was alone and lost again, unsure what to do.

But I had to keep living, and for that, I needed money. I thought about stealing something or robbing someone, but that went against everything angels stood for.

Or should have stood for.

I didn't know what was going on in Elysium these days, if angels were still considered righteous, honorable, pure.

I ended up in Phoenix, where the weather wasn't bad in March. I found a fight club.

Like the first time in Houston with Mr. Green, I was laughed at and ignored.

"A tiny thing like you," a bull of a man said from inside the cage. "What are you going to do? Stand there and look cute?"

Oh, that had boiled my blood.

Intent on proving myself, I scaled the cage's fence, and jumped in the ring. "I'm going to whip your ass, and if I do, I'll get all of your winnings for the night. Deal?"

The guy glanced at the suited man on a viewing deck upstairs. The man nodded, and the guy charged at me.

I was short and lean, but I was damn fast and a trained warrior who had fought against numerous supernaturals.

This man was a slow human.

I easily dodge all of his strikes, jumped out of the way when he lunged at me, and even toyed with him. Once, I slid underneath his legs and kicked him in the lower back, making him lose his balance. Another time, I climbed over his side and around him, wrapped my legs around his thick waist and my arms around his neck. The man fell back, thinking he would pin me. But I let him go and whirled out of the way. When he fell to the floor, the breath whooshed out of his lungs. I straddled him and landed a punch to his cheek, and another to his chin.

When he rose to his feet, he was furious.

But little by little, he tired.

And I won the fight.

As expected, the owner of the fighting club found me as I was leaving and invited me to fight tomorrow night.

"Whatever you made today from Tod, I'll guarantee double if you win," he promised.

I was in.

As I left the club, I felt dirty. Beating up humans to make money wasn't what an angel's life was supposed to be. If only Adona saw me now ...

I shook my head. Adona was what humans called the almighty god with a big G, but humans believed their God saw all, knew all. It wasn't exactly like that, and I was glad.

Not that I knew what was happening up there. Was Adona still in charge? Did she know about Rhodes and his betrayal? Was he working for her?

Those questions ate at my mind, and sometimes I could barely breathe.

I pulled the hood of my leather jacket up, shoved my hands in the pockets, and crossed the street. Three blocks from the club, I hopped on a bus, sat in the back row, and stared at the night outside the windows.

All the while, I watched everyone who got on and off the bus. I couldn't help it, knowing the angels were still after me and had issued a reward for any supernatural who captured me.

The bus ride to the edge of town, where I had been renting a room at a shady motel, was about twenty minutes, but it felt like four hours. I had been filled with so much anxiety since I had gotten my wings back.

I could have hidden in a dark alley near the fighting club, sprung my wings, and flown to the motel, but I had done that in another town before stopping in Phoenix, and supernaturals had easily spotted me.

Now, I avoided flying.

The more human I looked, the better.

That was why I had dyed my silver-blond hair dark brown—the color didn't take well, and it now looked like a dark, faded blond. But at least now my hair didn't advertise what I was.

After the ordeal with Levi, I had gone back to Houston to pack some of my things and get rid of my apartment. For a split second, I almost stopped by Sylvie's to say goodbye to her, but I knew she would tattle on me to an annoying demon.

Halfway through the ride, two tall men entered the bus. I tensed. One was wearing a loose tank, and his big biceps were covered in tattoos. The other wore a sleeveless hoodie and kept his head low.

They glanced at me, then sat in the middle of the bus.

Oh, shit.

Since I had lost my magic, I couldn't recognize all supernaturals, and lately it seemed I was either paranoid, or the ability was leaving me altogether, because I couldn't tell anymore.

I would only be sure the moment they attacked me.

As the bus rolled down the street, I wondered if I should exit at the next stop. Better to have them follow me now than near the motel.

Either way, if I had been found, I would have to move, but I needed my things from the motel, especially the potions that muted my aura from the angels. I had gone through a whole ordeal to get those and I couldn't lose them now.

Next stop was a busy one, near a school and an open shopping center, so it wasn't the best one to get off to fight supernaturals. The bus stopped, the men glanced at me, as if watching to see if I would get off. Instead, three teenagers and an elderly couple got on. They sat in the back of the bus, on the opposite side of me. They smiled while playing with their phones and two of them seemed to be sharing the same pair of earbuds. The older couple sat with difficulty a little farther back than the two men, and like me, they watched the outside as the bus started moving again.

The two men looked my way again.

The next stop was also not a good one, right by a hospital and a busy intersection.

Nearing the third stop, I got up and headed to the middle of the bus where the exit door was located. The bus slowed down, and I dared glance at the men—they were staring intently at me.

Shit.

The bus stopped, I hopped off, and started walking fast to the left, away from the hospital and into a more residential neighborhood. I glanced at the bus as it drove past me—and the two men were still inside and looking at me.

What?

I was about to run, but it seemed I didn't need to.

"Oh, angel," a voice called from behind me.

A cold shiver rolled down my spine and I tensed.

Slowly, I turned and saw the two girls and the boy who had been seated at the back with me.

Oh, shit, they were supernaturals.

Not wanting to find out what kind, I turned and ran—only to skid to a stop three seconds later.

The elderly couple stood in my path, only four feet from me.

"Where do you think you're going?" the man asked. Right before my eyes, they changed into younger versions of themselves with long, brown hair and pointed ears.

Wood fae.

It had been a glamour.

I whirled back to the teenagers. Were they fae too? No, two of them bared their fangs at me, and the other shifted into a hyena.

Five against one.

I couldn't fight five supernaturals by myself.

I pushed the desperation threatening to spill from me back down. Pumping my arms hard, I ran straight forward, into the road, leaving them behind.

I needed to cross the road, get out of sight, and then I could use my wings.

But I knew I couldn't outrun any of them.

I tried holding on until I crossed the line of buildings and entered a dark alley, but a vampire lunged at me from behind as I hit the sidewalk.

I didn't think. My wings sprang free and I pushed up.

Vines sprouted from the ground, through the broken cement, like a viper, and wrapped around my legs. I flapped my wings harder, but the vines pulled me down.

Then the hyena jumped over me, the vampires had their hands around me, and the fae walked like they were on the red carpet, a few feet back, enjoying the show.

"I've heard of your black wings," one of the fae said. "I thought it was only rumor."

"That means you're evil now?" the other fae asked. "Is that why the angels offered such a big reward for you?"

I wouldn't give them the satisfaction of answering their questions.

Instead, I opened my wings wide, turned them sideways, and spun my body in place. The fae were able to get away from the swipe, but the vampires and the hyena fell to the ground.

Without wasting a second, I flapped my wings and took to the sky.

Not three seconds later, I cried as a sharp pain exploded in my shoulder. I shook in the air, almost hitting the third floor of the building in front of me and had to swallow a cry when I looked down and saw a wooden stake protruding from my skin.

The damn thing hurt!

I tried ignoring the pain, but it was close to my shoulder blade and it was hard to flap and keep steady with that thing across my shoulder.

I tried landing on top of the building, and fell on my knees, breathing hard.

My trembling fingers brushed the stake, trying to pull it out, but couldn't get a grip on the smooth wood. Besides, if I really thought about it, depending on how bad it was, I could bleed out right here, right now.

With a groan, I pushed to my feet. I needed to soar from the roof, into the quiet neighborhood ahead. That should give me a good advantage against these supernaturals and I could get away.

I hoped.

I dragged my feet to the edge of the building and—

"Where do you think you're going, angel?" a voice said.

I glanced back and saw the two guys from the bus. So, they were supernaturals! Not that that mattered right now. I needed to get away from here.

I opened my wings, wincing in pain, and jumped.

And one of them jumped on top of me.

I screamed, tried holding the extra weight, but went down several yards away from the building, in a wooded area—was it a backyard? A park? I didn't know.

I fell hard on the grass, rolling several times, and even though I tucked my wings around myself, I felt my elbows and knees scrapping and burning against the lawn.

Dazed, I tried getting up, to continue moving, but everything hurt.

A growl came from above me and I found the man straddling me. Now that his hood had fallen from over his head, I could see his features and he was definitely a half goblin.

He bared his sharp teeth at me. "Behave, angel, or I'll have to turn in your dead body to them. The reward is smaller if you're dead."

What?

I groaned and pushed my hips up, as hard as I could. The half goblin rose a little, and I used that to pull one of my legs from underneath him. When he fell again, ready to strike, I kicked him in the stomach and he fell back.

"You—"

I kicked again, but this time he dodged my assault, and I crawled to the side and away. But I didn't go three feet until he was on top of me again. I dug my hands into the grass and fisted some dirt before he grabbed me by my hair and pulled me up to my knees.

"I'll skin you alive, angel."

I raised my hands and threw the dirt in his face, and I looked down, so the dirt wouldn't fall on me.

The half goblin sputtered and dropped me.

I wobbled to my feet.

The other man stood right in front of me. "Stop running, princess. You won't win." He grabbed my upper arm and pulled me along with him. Light, I wanted to cry. "Quick, the others are coming."

Wait. They weren't all together?

As if the universe wanted to answer my question, the two vampires zoomed to us—one taking the man holding me, the other grappling with the half goblin.

For a moment, I was free.

I ran, fleeing into a thicket. My ankle twisted on a raised tree root and I toppled to the ground.

Tonight was not my night.

If only I could survive ...

But as the time ticked by, the pain increased, my mind became blurrier, and the odds seemed to be against me.

I could hear the hyena coming at me. I found a thick branch on the ground, and when it lunged, I swung, hitting it with the branch square in its head. It went down with a yelp and was clearly disoriented.

I pushed through the pain, the dizziness, and kept going, one twisted step in front of the other. Finally, the trees opened up a little. My wings sprang wide and I took flight.

The hyena bit down on my wing and weighed me down. I yelped as I lost my balance and hit my wounded shoulder against a tree, and I almost went down again.

The hyena let go of me and I flew higher, until I was free

of the trees. I could hear the shouts and the fight below, but I didn't care.

I didn't care if a human saw me now.

All I had to do was fly.

Fly away, fly to the motel, and sleep this exhaustion off.

At some point, I could have sworn I had fainted while flying, but I was probably on automatic pilot, and somehow ended up at the door of my motel room.

I fumbled with the keys, my hands shaking hard, and I dragged myself inside. I kicked the door closed and fell to the floor, not even making it to the bed.

The adrenaline was leaving my body, and the pain was almost unbearable. I lifted my hand to the stake still in my shoulder, and my fingertips became red with my blood.

Shit, this wasn't good.

I sat up, my back to the bed, and tried to slow my breathing. I couldn't sleep now. If I did, I wasn't sure I would wake up.

I looked around, searching for a miracle. Some magical pain medicine or healing powder.

Three gold coins sat piled beside my bag on the dresser.

I blinked, feeling my consciousness slipping away.

Without a choice, I snatched one of the coins and called to her.

"Lacey," I whispered.

A moment later, a purple portal appeared in front of me and a pretty witch crossed.

"Ariella?" I heard her, but I couldn't really see more than a shape. "By the moon." She hissed and reached for me.

And everything went black.

2

———————

I WOKE UP WITH A START, BUT I COULDN'T EVEN SIT UP, because my shoulder hurt like a bitch. I groaned and lay back in bed.

"Hey, easy now." Lacey leaned over me in bed and help me prop up the pillows so I was half sitting.

I frowned for a second and then it all came back to me.

The supernaturals, the fight, the stake in my shoulder, the coins on the dresser, me calling for Lacey.

Shit.

I glanced down at myself. My shirt was cut above my breasts, revealing most of my blood-stained bra, and a bandage covered my shoulder. "Is it too bad?"

"Not anymore." She sat down on the edge of the bed. "If you hadn't called me, though." She shook her head. "but just so you know, when I healed you, the dye in your hair faded completely."

I reached to the ends of my hair and sure enough, the silver-blond was back. "Shit."

"What happened?" she asked, her tone concerned.

"What do you think? It's the damn reward. The entire supernatural world is after me."

"That's not true."

"All right. Then ninety-nine-point-ninety-nine percent." One corner of her lips tugged up and that reminded me so much of her brother. I cleared my dry throat. "Lacey, look, thank you for coming, and I'm really sorry I brought you here, but you can go now. You don't need to babysit me."

Her brows slammed down. "You don't get to do that. You called me and now I'm staying until I make sure you're okay."

"I'm okay."

"You're the patient. I'm the healer. I'll tell you when you're okay."

"Lacey—"

"Don't Lacey me," she said with a snap, the harshest she had ever talked to me. She rose to her feet. "It's midmorning, so I'm going out to get us some breakfast."

She headed to the door.

"Lacey." She glanced at me, ready to cut me off again. "Hm, I don't think you should go out like that."

She was wearing a black gown, fit for a witch. People would think she was dressed for Halloween in March ... or supernaturals in the area would know what she was.

"Oh." She glanced at my bag on the dresser. "You know what's the worst part of portaling in a rush?"

"No."

"Never having any of my stuff with me." She showed me her cell phone in her hand. "At least I was holding this."

Yeah, that could be inconvenient. I pointed my chin to my bag. "Help yourself."

There wasn't much in my bag. Since I left her and her

brother two weeks ago, I had bought two new leggings and three sweaters, since I kept getting them ruined. I looked down at the one I was wearing now, bloody, ripped, and now purposely cut. It seemed I would need more clothes soon.

Lacey changed into black leggings and a thin burgundy sweater, grabbed some of my money, and left the room.

I was left alone with my thoughts.

Why the hell had I called her here? Now she knew where I was, and she could tell her brother.

And what? Why would she tell her brother? Why would he care where I was? Why did I care if he knew where I was? That chapter of my life was over. He had tricked me, I had gotten what I asked for, and now it was all done.

My irritation grew and I felt restless.

I was hurt again and I had a fight tonight ... how would I be able to fight and make money like this? I had to figure something out.

Half an hour later, Lacey came back with a white bag and two to-go cups, which reminded me of the times her brother had brought food to me.

Why was I thinking about him again?

I shook my head once, tried scooting more upright against the pillows, and thanked her when she handed me a breakfast burrito and one of the cups.

"Everything okay?" I asked before I took a bite.

"Yeah," she said, sitting on the armchair beside the bed. I imagined she had spent most of the time there, watching over me. Poor thing. "I didn't see any supernaturals. And if they are close by, they can't sense us." I raised one eyebrow. "Last night, after I got your bleeding under control and managed to close your wound, I warded the room. It's not as strong as when Heidi does it, but it should work for now."

That reminded me. "How's Heidi?"

A soft smile adorned Lacey's lips. "She's better. I convinced her of doing a strengthening potion for herself for once, and I think it's helping." Her smile faded away. "It won't cure her arthritis, or slow down her aging, but it definitely helps."

"That's good." Heidi had been nothing but kind to me. She deserved the best.

"What about you?" Lacey asked. "I mean, obviously, not doing so well right now." She gestured to my shoulder. "But overall ... are you okay?"

"Yeah, I'm okay," I said automatically.

She didn't buy it. "Be honest, Ariella."

I shrugged, and then groaned in pain. "Shit."

Lacey got up, dropped her half-eaten burrito on the nightstand and placed her hands over my shoulder. A warm sensation flowed into me, coating my shoulder with numbness, and I sighed in relief.

"Better?"

I nodded. "A lot. Thanks."

She sat back down. "You've got your wings now, your revenge against the demon who took them, what now? Are you looking for your magic?"

I flinched when she mentioned the demon.

That was her damn father.

"Lacey, about Molraz. I'm so sorr—"

"Don't you dare say you're sorry." Her voice was harsh. "He was a terrible father, a terrible person. I can't say I had any good feelings toward him."

"But he was still your father."

"He was and that was the extent of it. Besides, what are you apologizing for? Levi was the one who killed him, not you."

Because of me. Levi had killed his father to save me.

I opened my mouth to ask about him but closed it again. The bond was broken, Levi was out of my life, and that was how it was supposed to be.

I placed a hand on my chest, where I felt a little sliver of something stirring every time I thought of him. What the hell was this? Me being a girly girl and feeling what I shouldn't for the bad boy? This was ridiculous.

"I'm not looking for my magic because I don't know where to start," I answered her question.

I had talked to Hazel two days ago, and she had said that she and Khalisa were still researching, but apparently their information on angels' magic was limited. They knew the theory of several spells to restore hidden magic, to make it strong, more stable ... all for witches. Besides, my magic wasn't suppressed.

It was gone.

She finished her breakfast and looked out the window—a small crack in the curtains revealed the day was bright and probably warm. Lacey returned her blue eyes to mine. "I can't guarantee anything, but I know a place where we could go to find some answers."

I perked up. "What do you mean?"

"It's a place most supernaturals think was lost centuries ago, but it wasn't. It's called the Grand Eternity Hall. It's like a library, a gallery, a museum, and a bank-slash-safe for magic and everything about it."

I frowned. I had heard about the Grand Eternity Hall. It had been a short paragraph in a book in one of my history classes. But I remembered thinking about it like the Library of Alexandria for humans. The biggest, most complete library and museum for any magical item and book on Earth. The place was hidden, only a few could access it, and it was secure.

Until one day, centuries ago, the Princes of the Underworld decided they could raid it, steal all the magical artifacts, and use them for themselves, and it ended in a big, bloody battle. It was said the Grand Eternity Hall prevailed, sans a few items the demons were able to steal, and because of that, had restricted access to all supernaturals.

If the place still existed, it had been hidden and silent for too long.

"I've heard of it," I whispered.

"Really? Most supernaturals haven't. I mean, maybe super old vampires, and some powerful witches, if they were alive back then."

"You said you know this place."

She nodded. "I can go there anytime I want."

I stared at her, incredulous. "How?"

She shrugged. "They are fond of me."

That still didn't answer my question. How were they fond of her? How did they meet her in the first place? Who was they?

"And you can go there?"

"Yes, and I think they would be okay with me bringing you." She placed a hand in her pockets. "Do you want to go there?"

"Of course!" Even if this place didn't lead to anything,

what did I have to lose? Nothing! Lacey slipped her hand out of her pocket and showed me a silver coin. "It's just like the golden ones."

"Yeah, I've learned the spell for the coins." She stood up and reached for me. "You should change before we go."

Right. My shirt was still caked with dried blood and I probably smelled pretty bad. With Lacey's help, I took off my clothes, took a quick shower, careful not to wet the bandages, got dressed in leggings and a thin sweater, and shoved my feet in my boots.

Lacey picked up my bag and slung it over her shoulder. "Ready?"

I nodded. "Ready."

She pressed on the silver coin and a white portal appeared by our side. She stepped through first and I followed.

The portal opened to a large, beautiful front yard, with stone paths and flanked by tall trees and colorful flowers, which led to a two-story house with brown siding and a wrap-around porch. White curtains covered the windows, but the lights were on in every room.

I frowned. "This doesn't look like the Grand Eternity Hall."

Lacey smiled at me. "First, have you ever seen a picture or drawing of the hall?" I shook my head. "Second, they had to change things a bit when they decided to come out of hiding."

"They came out of hiding?"

"They tried." She started heading toward the house. "Come on. I'll show you around."

This couldn't be right.

The Grand Eternity Hall wasn't a small house in the middle of the woods. Was it?

Lacey opened the front door and smiled at me.

I paused at the door and gawked at the interior. This was another place completely. I glanced back to the porch. Very rustic, very traditional, and very small.

I walked in, taking in inch by inch of the giant, earthy room. I was in what could only be described as a lobby of a spectacular place. The floors were smooth gray marble and the walls were covered in vines and leaves.

Small iron sconces jutted out from between the vines, each holding a thick white candle. A big dome of colorful stained glass sat atop the ceiling, which was at least three stories high. A round, wooden circle floated halfway to the dome, holding several burning white candles.

The light coming from the dome gave the place an eerie, enchanted air.

What seemed like roots or thick vines twisted around archways, two to the right, two to the left, and one in the back, right beside the wide stone staircase that led upstairs to a balcony that wrapped around the entire lobby—and all of the railing was simply twisted vines and a few leaves.

"I know that feeling," Lacey said, watching me. "I was in awe the first time I came here too. To be honest, I'm always in awe of this place."

"It's amazing," I said, still shocked.

She chuckled. "And this is just the lobby. Wait until you see the rest. If you get to see it all. I don't think I even know every room and corner of this place. Come on."

I followed Lacey to the archway beside the staircase. It

followed the same pattern of the lobby, with vines and roots everywhere, sconces and candles between the archways.

As we walked, I noticed the candles flicking on as we approached them, and off as we walked away.

"The candles are enchanted," I said, amused.

"Yeah, the hall is all enchanted. The Evermores say the hall has a mind and magic of its own."

The Evermores. The moment Lacey said it, I remembered reading about them in that short paragraph—they were the family appointed to take care of the hall several millennia ago.

"They are still alive?" I asked, looking side to side into the archways.

This bit reminded me of Duncan's house: beyond the archways were rooms with artifacts and items on display, like an art gallery.

"Oh, the Evermores are witches and warlocks, and they age like us, though I do think they live longer normal witches."

I paused in front of one archway and stared at a mirror with a golden frame. There was no reflection in the mirror, just a foggy haze, like thick clouds obscuring the view.

"I thought the items were supposed to be tucked away and protected." From the harm they could do if they ended up in the wrong hangs.

"The items in this gallery aren't dangerous," Lacey said. "The dangerous one are locked away deep in the hall." She looked at me with huge eyes. "That reminds me, you probably won't need your potions here."

"What do you mean?"

"This entire place is warded and hidden from any supernatural. Unless you know about it, unless you're invited in by the Evermores, or someone brings you in, you have no way of finding it."

"That's good." Since I had a proven track of forgetting to take my potions, this was great news.

"I thought you would like it." She nudged my arm. "Let's keep going."

At the end of the long hall were two giant wooden doors with lots of carvings. If I didn't know this place was full of magic, I would say Lacey and I would never be able to open those doors by ourselves.

But as it was, the doors opened when we approached them.

And once more I was shocked into silence at how stunning the place was.

The library was even taller than the lobby, with a stained-glass dome that was at least twice as big, and right under it was an arched tall wooden counter, and a huge tree with thick, twisted trunk, and vivid green leaves.

I didn't need to be supernatural to know this tree was ancient and powerful.

"They will be here," Lacey said, walking around the counter.

With slow steps, I followed her.

Behind the tree were a few rows of long tables, and at the end, a huge stained-glass wall, similar to the dome, and to the sides of the tables were rows and rows of shelves and books that reached the tall ceiling, with vines and roots and leaves everywhere. Knotted staircases dotted the place, leading up and up. In two levels, the staircase led to coves with small sitting areas beside the stained-glass wall.

And here and there were the same silver sconces and candles I had seen outside.

"Thank goodness the candles are enchanted," I muttered. With books and wood, this place would burn in seconds.

"Everything in here is enchanted," a voice said.

I turned back to the tables and saw an image I didn't know how I had missed before: four beautiful young witches that looked like quadruplets, despite the obvious age difference, and four animals—an orange cat on the table, a green snake twisted on a chair, and a raven perched on a rail.

"Hi, girls," Lacey said, walking up to them. "I hope you don't mind. I brought a friend who needs help."

The witches all stared at me.

"Hi," I said, feeling silly. "I'm Ariella."

"Nice to meet you, Ariella," the oldest one said. She had long, chestnut brown hair and deep blue eyes. "I'm Abigail, and these are my sisters: Magnolia,"—she gestured to the next in line, with light brown hair and green eyes—"Gwendolyn." She pointed to a young girl with dark-brown hair and green eyes. "And Brittany." She beckoned to the last one, the youngest, with light brown hair and hazel eyes.

They all waved at me politely.

Lacey scoffed. "We call them Abbie, Maggie, Gwen, and Britt."

"We're the protectors of the Grand Eternity Hall," Abbie said.

"You are," Britt muttered. Everyone shifted their gazes to her. "Well, she is. The eldest is the one who inherits the hall."

Abbie looked at her youngest sister. "We already talked about this, Britt, and I would love if you could refrain from arguing in front of others."

"You can't do this alone, blah blah blah," Britt said. She rose from her chair, grabbing a thick, leather-bound book from the table. "We've heard that a million times." She stomped away and disappeared among two tall bookshelves.

"I apologize for her behavior," Abbie said to me. "She's fourteen and is definitely in her rebel teenage years."

"I didn't have a rebel teenage phase," Maggie said.

"Mom and dad were alive for most of your teenage years," Gwen said.

"Girls," Abbie snapped softly. She looked pointedly at me. "Lacey said she brought you for help. What can we help you with?"

My mind was spinning and I had so many questions ...

Where were their parents? Was Abbie in charge? She looked younger than me. What was that about the eldest inheriting the Hall? Were they alone in this endless place? Did they ever leave and mix up with the human world?

Whoa, my thoughts went on and on ...

The snake moved on the chair and I stilled.

I stared at the snake, afraid of moving.

"Don't worry, he doesn't bite," Maggie said. "The tiger isn't here at the moment, but when you see him, don't let his size scare you. He's a softie."

I blinked.

There was a freaking tiger.

"Oh, you don't know their names," Gwen said. "The snake is Venom, the cat is Merlin, the raven is Bane, and the tiger is Rune. All males."

I stared at her, sure I would forget their names in three seconds.

I shook my head once, trying to focus. Abbie had asked me a question. What I needed help with.

"I lost—"

The words faded away as a man appeared from among two bookshelves, the opposite side from where Britt had gone, holding an open book in his hands. "I found it."

He looked up from the book, his eyes met mine, he halted, and his shoulders tensed.

"Ariella ... what are you doing here?"

3

———

I spun to Lacey, fuming. "You didn't tell me your brother was here."

She raised both her hands. "I didn't know!"

It was too much of a coincidence.

"Take me back," I demanded, irritation igniting in my chest. "I want to go back."

"But what about your magic? You came here for your magic."

As if my eyes had a life of their own, they shifted to Levi. He had walked forward and dropped the book on the table, right beside the witches, but his attention was still turned to us.

By the light, the demon looked dashing in a dark gray suit that hugged his big shoulders. His face was as sharply handsome as I remembered, with chiseled corners and bright blue eyes.

My gaze flicked to his full lips and I couldn't help remembering what he had done with them. My body instantly heated up and I suppressed a hitched breath. My chest hurt with sudden want. Thankfully, the bond was broken and he couldn't feel my burning desire.

What the hell? I shouldn't feel anything other than contempt and anger toward him. He was an evil demon who had used me.

How many times would I have to repeat that for it to stick in my mind?

Thousands, it seemed.

His gaze moved to my neck, where the bandage peeked from under the collar of my sweater. I thought I saw his eyes darken, but it could have been my imagination.

Levi shifted his weight, turned to the witches, and pointed to the books.

I let out a long breath.

I could do this. We were adults. For whatever reason he was here, I didn't care. Hopefully, he would be done soon and leave. Or the witches would be able to help me and I would walk out of here quickly.

It didn't matter.

What mattered was my magic.

"Fine," I muttered. I puffed up my chest and faced the witches.

But they were talking to Levi in hushed tones.

My irritation made itself front and center again, and I clenched my fists, wishing I could punch him and send him to the underworld.

Noticing me, Gwen shushed them. Then they all looked at me. Even the cat seemed to wake up long enough to glance at me.

Not containing myself, I looked at Levi. "Will you leave if I ask you to?"

He opened his mouth to answer, but Abbie beat him to the punch. "Levi is an honored guest at the Grand Eternity Hall, and he won't be going anywhere."

Honored guest? I almost scoffed at that. What could he have possible done to be awarded such a title?

Honestly, I didn't want to know.

So, I did my best to ignore him and continued, "Lacey brought me here because she thought you could help me get my magic again."

Maggie frowned. "Is it suppressed?"

I shook my head and told her what had happened—during a battle, a former Prince of the Underworld had absorbed my magic and left me with nothing.

Not even an ounce.

Now that I had my wings back, I could feel a tiny sliver of magic, the one that made it possible for me to make them disappear inside of me as if they were the size of my palm instead of ten feet wide.

But as much as I tried, I couldn't access that magic.

"And if it means I'll allocate that magic to somewhere else, I would rather not mess with it," I said.

"Understandable," Abbie said. "That sounds complicated. I don't think we have many books about angel magic."

"We were always secretive creatures," I said.

She nodded. "Exactly." Beside her, Levi sat down and perused the book he had found, as if nothing was happening here. "But the knowledge in this library is endless. I'm positive we can find something. If not the exact answer you're looking for, then a clue or some direction."

I perked up. "That would be great."

"It might take a while," Abbie said. She pointed to the

books spread over the table. "We're working on something important right now, and probably won't be done today."

My chest deflated. But I had been without my magic for over six months, hadn't I? What was a few more hours? "That's fine," I lied. "So, hm, should I leave and come back tomorrow or—"

Abbie stood. "If Lacey brought you here, then you're a friend. You should stay here for the night. I promise that tomorrow we can at least discuss more of your situation and decide."

Stay in this place with Levi ... it wasn't ideal, but what was nowadays? Go back to that shitty motel, spend money on it, hide from the supernaturals looking for me?

It was safer here.

"That would be great," I said.

"Good." Abbie gestured to my side. "Then Myg here will take you to a guest bedroom now."

I glanced to where Abbie was pointing and almost yelped when I saw a short female goblin standing five feet behind me. A small creature that came up to my waist, with pale green skin, huge, pointed ears, flimsy dark hair, and a scrunched ugly face. She wore a simple black dress with a white apron over it.

"This way," Myg said, her voice scratching like old bark.

The goblin shuffled from the room. I hesitated, a little confused by this turn of events. All I wanted was to find a spell to give me back my magic, and leave this place, preferably today. Was that too much to ask?

I let out a sigh and followed the goblin as she went back to the lobby and up the stairs. We turned right and went down a set of wide hallways that turned and turned and then turned again. Occasionally, we passed lofts with comfy chairs and small tables, set where the hallways intersected. By the fifth turn and the third sitting area, I was definitely lost.

This place was huge. Beautiful, but endless.

Finally, Myg stopped in the middle of a long hallway and opened double wooden doors. "Please, come in."

I walked in and like any other room in this hall, this bedroom took my breath away. It was a large rectangular room with a sitting area to the right, and the bed to the left. Vines and roots crawled up the walls, and the furniture was knotted wooden branches. The cushions and bedding were white and light blue, matching the curtains, which were half closed over the set of tall windows along the opposite wall.

"The bathroom and the closet are that way." Myg gestured to a small archway on the left, past the four-poster bed. "There should be toiletries and clothes, but if anything is missing, you can press this button,"—she pointed to a small green button beside the door—"and I'll come to assist you." Her words were polite, but it sounded like a rehearsed script.

"Thank you," I whispered, still feeling like I couldn't process all of this. I walked to the window and looked out. I couldn't see the rest of the building, just lots trees, some as tall as the window.

For some reason, it felt like this place was like Elysium—easily accessible by portals, but not really on Earth. A magical place, alive in another dimension.

"Supper is served in the family's dining room at 5 o'clock," Myg said.

I frowned. "And where is the fam—"

The words died on my lips when I turned and didn't see

her there. The door was closed and the goblin was nowhere to be seen.

Apparently, when it was time for supper, I should probably leave the room early, because I was sure to get lost.

I glanced at my phone. There was no signal, as I expected, but the rest was still working, and the digital clock told me it was only two in the afternoon. Could I explore this place? No, I would probably get lost. What I could do, then? Rest? Check the bandage?

I walked through the archway and found the large closet filled with clothes—and guess what? Everything in here was my size. Gotta love magic—and the bathroom, with a long vanity, two sinks, a standing shower, and a clawfoot bathtub.

Knowing I needed to relax a little, I opted for a long bath in scalding hot water.

It took me longer than I would admit to redo my bandage and get dressed again after my delicious bath. It hurt a lot too, but thankfully the wound was healing well, thanks to Lacey's magic, and I was able to put a smaller bandage on the front of my shoulder.

The cabinets underneath the bathroom sink had all I needed, including a first aid kit.

It was amazing.

For my clothes, I almost picked something I had brought over, but opted to check out the closet instead. I found nightgowns, graphics tees, suits, elegant gowns, and everything in between.

I picked black leggings, a boat-neck loose teal sweater, and put on my worn combat boots.

At four thirty, I left the room and turned left from where Myg and I had come before. I was sure my first turn was right, my second too, but on the third, I wasn't sure anymore.

I knew this would happen and I couldn't even call Lacey to come and find me, because phones didn't work here. So, I just kept going, hoping to bump into someone or find a place I recognized.

I turned another corner and found myself in a wide corridor like the one downstairs with all the artifacts. Another gallery.

I slowed down, glancing side to side, taking in the items. Most of them meant nothing to me. A beautiful sword, a broken one, some sparkling jewels, a huge red ring, a silver comb, a heavy cross pendant, a large bow and a quiver with arrows, a piece of armor ...

But what made me stop was a beautiful white and silver harp, taller than me. I walked into the gallery and rounded the harp. It looked so much like the one Adona had. She loved playing it whenever we had special events and fancy dinners.

I ran my fingers over the strings and sighed.

What I wouldn't give to know what was going on back home. Was Adona safe? Was she plotting with Rhodes? Did she send him to retrieve the Scarlet Hex Blade and kill us all? But why? What was the end goal here?

I couldn't begin to guess.

I felt impotent. I had gotten my wings; I was going to get my magic back somehow, but I was still in the dark, and that scared me.

"You're lost."

I froze, my fingertips on the chords. Slowly, I lowered my hand and turned to the voice.

Levi.

My heart tugged at the sight of him. He hadn't changed since I last saw him a couple of hours ago, but he had lost the tie and undone the top two buttons of his shirt.

More causal, but still hot as hell.

"Have you been following me?" I asked.

He shoved his hands in his pants' pockets. "No, sweetheart. I was on my way from my bedroom to the dining room for supper, and this is my path."

"That's not what I meant." I crossed my arms. "I mean here. In the Grand Eternity Hall. You knew I was coming."

"How would I have known that, sweetheart? I've been here for a couple of days."

"Why are you here? And how come you're an honored guest of the Grand Eternity Hall?"

One corner of his lips tugged up in that same charming smile of his. "Aren't we curious?"

I clamped my mouth, ashamed I couldn't hold my tongue. Something about him messed with me. I wanted to be indifferent to him, to show him his betrayal didn't affect me.

I even thought I was exaggerating. Was it a betrayal? He set out to get me from the start, and he was always cold and telling me to keep my distance.

I was the one who read too much into all of it. And yet, I couldn't stop the wild thoughts in my mind.

"I'm serious, can't you come back after the witches help me?" It was a bold question, I knew that, but I couldn't help it.

Levi strolled closer and halted two feet from me.

I wanted to take a step back, but I wouldn't give him the satisfaction of seeing me squirming.

He leaned closer and locked his blue eyes on mine. "Do I bother you that much, sweetheart?" His gaze slid down my neck, my shoulder, and down the rest of my body, darkening. "Is it annoyance, or something else?" I shoved his chest and he chuckled. "You make it too easy to tease you."

"You're impossible."

He winked at me, then walked away. "If you don't want to get lost again, come with me."

I would rather be lost for the next three days than follow him.

But to contradict me, my stomach growled. Embarrassed, I pressed a hand to my belly and followed the demon out of the gallery.

The moment I stepped foot back into the hallway, something big and dark jumped at me, pushing me back.

I yelled as I fell and hit my head hard on the floor.

I blinked fast, trying to fight the black spots in my visions, and all I saw were the sharp teeth snapping inches from my face.

4

BOLTS OF DARKFIRE HIT THE MONSTER'S FACE AND BODY, AND IT scurried away from me. The thing crawled on the ceiling, perched upside down, and snarled.

A harpy. It was a freaking harpy with birdlike wings for arms, talons for feet, and feathers for hair. It snarled at us, poised to attack.

Levi stood before me, a hand stretched toward the harpy, and the other to me. I grabbed his hand and let him help me up. The world revolved for two seconds, but I was able to keep my balance.

"A harpy? Loose in the hall?" I asked, confused. What was going on?

The harpy opened her wings, let out a screech, and lunged at us.

Ripples of shadow rose from the floor and tangled around the harpy. With its wings tied, it fell to the floor with a heavy thud. Levi tightened the shadows, then he produced a small mirror from his pocket, and pointed it at the harpy.

The creature screeched as it was sucked into the mirror in a whirlwind.

I stared at Levi, eyes wide, shocked.

He pocketed the mirror and turned to me. "That's why I'm here. Myg didn't lock the door of the prison wing last night after cleaning the hallway, and the creatures woke up and got away."

"You're saying evil monsters are loose in the hall?"

He nodded. "They can't get out of here, but they are hiding and attacking us when they can. I was asked to help the witches catch them and return them to their eternal sleep."

"The mirror is a prison."

"It's more like a police car. I'll release the harpy back into its dungeon, where it can't hurt anyone."

I looked up to where the harpy had been perched on the ceiling. I could see its talons' marks on the vines around the archways and walls. I had known many of the artifacts and books this place held were dangerous and evil ... but monsters? I had no idea there were monsters here.

"Did they hurt anyone yet?"

He shook his head. "Nothing critical so far."

"That's what Abbie meant when she said you were working on something important first."

"Yes. Keeping everyone safe in the hall is the priority right now."

I stared at him. I had seen him kill a demon who had been chained to a post, torture an angel, he had threatened me several times, trapped me in a witch's circle, and he had killed his own father.

What could be eviler?

And yet, here he was, helping the witches of the Grand Eternity Hall.

This man was contradiction on two legs.

"I know I'm handsome, sweetheart, but you can stop staring now." He winked at me and started down the hallway as if nothing had happened.

I huffed, annoyed, but followed him.

After a dozen turns—at least it had felt like that—we crossed another archway and walked into a large room with a long wooden table with knotted feet and twelve knotted chairs.

The four witches I had met before were here with Lacey, along with an older one, who was seated at the table's end.

"Ariella, this is Belinda, our grandmother," Abbie said as I approached them. Levi, though, rounded the table and took a seat beside his sister.

Belinda turned her milky white eyes to me. "Hm, an angel." She frowned. "But not quite. What's wrong, dear?"

Standing beside the table, I shifted my weight. "I recently recovered my wings, but I'm still deprived of my magic."

She offered me a wrinkled hand. "May I?"

I hesitated. I knew a bunch of witches, most of them were super nice, but there were plenty of wicked witches out there.

I slipped my hand in hers. She gripped it tight, closed her eyes, and hummed. I felt her power enveloping me and I gasped. She looked frail with white hair tied in a loose bun, and more wrinkles than any witch I had ever seen, but she was powerful.

"I see it was stolen," she whispered. "By a prince of the underworld. He's dead now, and your magic gone."

Why did it hurt to hear the truth out loud? Especially coming from a stranger?

She opened her eyes and dropped my hand. "Don't worry, dear, my granddaughters will do everything they can to help you."

"Thanks," I muttered.

Maggie patted the empty seat by her side and I went to her.

Belinda was on the end, with Abbie, Britt, Lacey, and Levi to her left. And on her right was one empty seat, then Gwen, Maggie, and me.

I was about to ask Maggie in a faint voice why the empty seat when two others entered the dining room—a middle-aged man and a young boy.

The man didn't say anything to anyone. He strolled to the other end of the table and took a seat. But the boy ran to Gwen and Maggie, who squeezed him tight.

"This is Trent, our brother," Maggie said with a smile. "He's ten."

"And that's our uncle," Gwen said. She had looked shy and quiet before, and now her voice was soft, as if she was afraid of speaking up.

"Uncle Magnus," Abbie started. "This is Ariella, our guest."

He nodded, his hazel eyes skimming through me as if I was a fly on the wall. "Is dinner ready?"

Myg popped beside him a second later. "Yes, sir." The goblin snapped her fingers, and suddenly, the table was set and covered plates appeared in front of us. She snapped her fingers again and the covers disappeared.

"Hm, calamari and shrimp puffs. My favorite," Trent said

from his seat between Belinda and Gwen. He dug in and everyone followed suit.

Even the animals who were in a special corner of the room with rugs and pillows, had their bowls and were eating their dinner. I saw the tiger's bowl, but no tiger.

Maggie followed my gaze. "You're wondering where Rune is? He's moody and prefers eating alone. He'll probably come when we're gone." She shoved two shrimp puffs into her mouth and smiled at me.

"Myg, where's the parsley?" Britt asked.

A small silver shaker with parsley popped beside her.

Levi told Abbie about the harpy and she mentioned going to the dungeon with him later to release the monster. Trent told something funny about one of his earlier lessons to Belinda, and she listened intently. Gwen told Britt to thank Myg, but the younger girl shrugged. Lacey started a conversation with Maggie about her latest vision.

I tried eating, but I couldn't help feeling overwhelmed. There was so much going on, so many people, so much liveliness ... I wasn't used to this anymore.

I had had something similar when I was in the Guardian Academy and had Rachel and Jeremiah. And even though my mother didn't like that I had gone to the academy, she was always protective of me, and my little sister saw me as a role model.

Then I experienced that here and there, with Farrah and Wyatt, with Kayden, the queen fae, and with the other supernaturals I had met over the years.

But it was always fleeting, like this one would be.

I looked up and found Levi watching me. My chest hurt at the intensity of his gaze. Why didn't he ignore me? It would be so much easier. I turned to Maggie and paid attention to her conversation.

"I don't know what it means," she said. "Everything was dark, but I could see oval-shaped stones, and fragments of white light inside them. Then the lights faded from the stones and floated together, forming one bright ball that spun in the air among the darkness."

"Hm, maybe you should read one of Mom's old diaries," Gwen suggested. "Some of her visions are detailed, and anytime she found out what they meant, she wrote it down."

"Visions?" I asked, curious.

"Oh yeah," Maggie said. "Each of us has a special gift, like something that make us different." She sounded excited about the topic. "Grandma has the gift of touching something and seeing some of their history and some of their future."

"She said you guys are going to be able to help me." That was promising.

"She said we're going to do everything we can to help you," Britt said from across the table. "That doesn't mean it'll work."

She was right and that sent a wave of sadness and frustration through me.

"But we will try," Maggie said. "That's what we do. Anyway, Abbie is gifted with plants. Being the eldest and the real protector of the Grand Eternity Hall, she is connected to the house more than any of us. When the hall allows, she can control the plants. And because of that affinity, she's really good with potions."

"And cooking," Trent said, licking his fingers after having devoured the appetizer. "She makes a great chocolate cake."

Everyone smiled at that.

"My gift is something like visions, or prophecies, depending on the severity of my visions," Maggie continued. "But not everything I see comes to fruition, and honestly, most of my visions make no sense whatsoever."

"I'm an empath," Gwen said, her voice low. "If I'm attuned to people, I can feel what they are feeling. But sometimes, when there are too many people around me, with too many strong emotions, it's hard to control. I feel it all."

"You'll learn to control it, Gwen," Abbie said, sounding like a mother, even though she couldn't be five years older than Gwen. "And when you do, you'll be able to block everything."

Gwen nodded, playing with the last piece of calamari on her plate.

"You'll also be able to control others' feelings," Maggie said, nonchalantly. Gwen glared at her. "What?"

"You know she doesn't like that," Abbie muttered.

"Then she can ignore that side of her gift," Britt said, sounding snarky, like she had earlier today.

"What about you?" I asked her.

The youngest of the girls regarded me as if considering if I was worth the answer. "I can see and talk to ghosts, and when I can, I help them pass over."

I frowned. I knew all light and dark witches could do something similar, but to this coven, or whatever they wanted to call it, doing that was an affinity. It was incredible how magic worked differently for each of us.

"Are there ghosts in here now?" I asked, joking.

"Not right now, but earlier I saw two passing by the hallway," she said, dead serious.

I straightened. There were ghosts in the Grand Eternity Hall? I mean ... why not, right?

"I can talk to animals," Trent said with a smile. He looked at Merlin, Bane, and Venom in the corner. "They already ate but want more food."

"They *always* want more food," Maggie said.

And everyone laughed.

Everyone expect Levi and Magnus.

"Speaking of food," Magnus started. "Myg, we're ready for the next course."

The goblin snapped her fingers and our plates were replaced by new ones with the same silver cover. She snapped again and the covers disappeared.

Seared steak dripping with butter, baked sweet potatoes full of brown sugar, and roasted asparagus. The smell alone made my mouth water.

For a full minute, the table was quiet as everyone started eating. I almost moaned at the melting steak and the perfectly seasoned side dishes. I hadn't eaten a meal like this in quite some time and I had to restrain myself to not attack my food and inhale it.

As I remembered our conversation, something came to me. "What about your uncle?" I asked Maggie in a hushed voice. "Does he have a gift?"

"If he touches someone, he can make them do or believe anything he says or thinks," she whispered. "If he tells you to jump off a cliff, you would, without hesitation."

I frowned. That was a dangerous gift. "That can be a useful gift during a battle."

"It didn't help us much during the last one," she said, a little louder.

"What about the last one?" Britt asked.

"The last battle," Maggie said.

"The one a couple of hundred years ago, right?" I asked, remembering what I had read about them before. "When the Grand Eternity Hall closed for good."

"That was the second to last," Gwen said.

What? There was another one?

"About ten years ago, our parents opened the hall again," Abbie told me. "It wasn't well known. They wanted to start slow, test the waters, help a few people here and there ... but six years ago, a higher demon came in. He pretended to be a half demon who had lost his family and was losing his magic." She shook her head. "The higher demon was Molraz."

I gasped and glanced at Levi and Lacey. Both of them looked down at their plates, but they weren't eating.

"He wanted a powerful artifact that was being kept safe in one of the most secure rooms in the hall," Maggie said. "The Scarlet Hex Dagger."

I almost choked on the piece of steak I was chewing. "What?"

I looked at the siblings again. Levi had brought his whiskey glass to his lips, and Lacey gave me a dreadful look.

"He brought in hundreds of demons," Gwen said, her voice low. "We weren't prepared."

"It was a horrible battle," Belinda said. "My son and his wife lost their lives, and I'm afraid that if a powerful higher demon hadn't come to help us, we all would have died." She stared straight at Levi. He emptied his whisky glass, set it down, and the amber liquid filled the glass again.

My jaw fell to the floor.

Levi had come to help the Grand Eternity Hall when his father attacked it?

"That's why Levi is an honored guest," I muttered.

Abbie nodded. "We owe him a lot."

"Molraz still escaped with the dagger," Levi said bitterly.

"But you saved my life," Abbie said.

"And mine," Trent said.

"Everyone's, really," Gwen added.

I frowned and had to hold my tongue from asking why. Why would a twenty-two-year-old higher demon help strangers and fight against his father? I knew he didn't like his father, but I doubted he had jumped in all of his father's battles.

It had to be because of the dagger.

He hadn't come for a noble cause. He had come for the dagger, and he had still lost it.

I glanced at him, seeing through his mask. Right now, he pretended to be a civilized, humane demon, but I knew the truth. Under all of that charm was cunning and malice. All he knew was how to use others for his gain.

He met my gaze for three seconds, then went for his whiskey again.

I still couldn't wrap my head around the fact that the Scarlet Hex Blade had been here for a long time before surfacing with Molraz. Rhodes must have known about the dagger and sent Molraz to retrieve it.

Not a few months later, I had taken the dagger from Molraz.

Maybe, just maybe, I could return it to the hall. It was probably more secure than where I had it hidden now. But it had been taken once already.

It could be taken again.

I frowned. "Does it happen often? Having artifacts stolen? I mean, probably not now since the hall is closed again."

"The hall isn't closed," Abbie answered. "Well, we closed for about a month while we grieved and made some changes, but we didn't want one attack to stop us. We're certainly open, but it's not widely known."

I wasn't expecting that.

"You didn't answer her question," Trent whispered.

Abbie nodded. "Right. No, it's not common. In fact, in our eight-thousand-year history, we've had only eleven artifacts and books stolen."

That was a good ratio.

"The hall has incredible magical protection," Maggie said. "For an artifact to be taken ... it takes a lot of planning and cunning. They would have to surprise and overwhelm us, and somehow neutralize the building's magic."

"But we have taken more precautions since the latest attack," Abbie said. "I would say it's nearly impossible to have an artifact stolen now."

"Hopefully, we won't have to test that theory," Gwen said.

Britt snorted. "Eventually, we will. We all know most supernaturals are greedy, power-hungry, and incredibly selfish."

Magnus cleared his throat. "Can we change the subject? I don't like gloomy with my dinner."

"Sorry, uncle," Maggie and Gwen said.

"You're the gloomy one, Magnus," Belinda said, her tone firmer.

He straightened in his chair. "Mind your own business, Belinda."

"Don't start, please," Abbie pleaded. She glanced at Myg and nodded.

As the dinner plates were replaced by dessert—a delicious, salted caramel cheesecake with pecans—I observed the family. I now knew the grandma was actually the mother of the girls' father, and Magnus had called Belinda by her name, not Mother. It could be that he was her son and called her that anyway, but after seeing the tension in their short exchange, I believed he was the brother of the girls' mother.

Not that it mattered. They were all family and took care of the Grand Eternity Hall.

I put the last piece of the cheesecake in my mouth, my belly already protesting. I had eaten too much, but damn, it was so good, I couldn't stop until everything was gone.

I reached for my glass of red wine—how Myg knew what I liked drinking, I had no idea—and almost spilled it when a loud roar echoed from the hallway.

Abbie, Levi, and Magnus jumped to their feet, magic at their fingertips, as they stared at the archway.

A moment later, a huge tiger ran inside. I gasped. I mean, I had known they had a tiger, but I hadn't expected to see it. Especially not like this, barreling inside the dining room as if his tail was on fire.

The tiger skidded to a stop, looked at Trent, and let out a long whine.

"He's hurt," Trent said.

The tiger collapsed on the floor.

5

———

IN A FLASH, EVERYONE WAS UP AND MOVING. TRENT, MAGGIE, and Lacey tended to the tiger, while Gwen and Britt stayed with their grandma. Abbie, Levi, and Magnus advanced to the doorway.

I went with them, though I couldn't do shit other than punch someone unconscious.

"Talk to me, Trent," Abbie said. White magic flickered in her hands, same as her uncle's, while Levi had a dozen darkfire stakes waiting to be thrown.

"He didn't see what attacked him," Trent said, his voice shaking. "It came from behind. He just knows it was one of the creatures that escaped the dungeon."

"Damn it," Abbie muttered.

I glanced back and saw Lacey press her hand to the tiger's bloody back and heal him. The other animals stayed with Belinda, Gwen, and Britt, as if they all needed to protect grandma.

Levi, Abbie, and Magnus walked into the hallway. I stood

under the archway, on the lookout as they spread out and searched for whatever was outside.

Five minutes later, they came back.

"Whatever it was, it's hidden again," Abbie said.

We walked into the dining room. Maggie hugged Trent.

Lacey finished. "He'll be fine," she said. "But he needs lots of rest."

Trent let out a long sigh and leaned down to hug the tiger.

"We tried being patient with these creatures, but they are testing us," Abbie said. "We should hunt them."

Magnus nodded. "Agreed."

"Myg, see that Grandma, Trent, Britt, and Gwen make it safely to Grandma's room," Abbie ordered.

The goblin nodded and started for Grandma.

"I want to help!" protested Gwen.

"Me too!" Britt wailed.

"This is not open for discussion," Abbie said. "Go with Grandma, and Trent, take the animals with you, and protect them all. Understood?"

They mumbled yes and exited through the back with Myg—Grandma holding tight to the girls' arms as she couldn't see.

"Should we divide into groups?" Lacey asked.

"I'll go with you," Maggie said. They had a similar demeanor and seemed close. Now looking at them side by side, I would guess that Maggie was nineteen years old, like Lacey.

"I'll go by myself," Magnus said, marching out of the dining room.

Abbie let out a breath and looked at me. "Sorry about him. He helps us a lot, but he's a pain in the ass to deal with."

Maggie snorted. "You can say that again."

"Anyway, Levi and I are the strongest, so it's best if we're separated," Abbie said. "I'll go by myself."

Levi looked at me, his blue eyes dark. "You should go to your room."

I placed my hands on my waist. "Why? Because I don't have my magic. Give me a goddamn sword and I can fight."

"I can get you a sword," Abbie said.

Levi groaned. "You should go with Abbie, then."

I glared at him.

"No." Abbie pointed to Levi and me. "Whatever is going on there, I want no part in it. I'll go by myself, and you two go together." She shoved her hand inside the pocket of her dress and pulled out a handful of pink stones. "Here. Send your magic to the stone if you're in trouble. It'll alert the others and guide you to them."

She handed us the stones. Levi took ours.

"What happens after?" Maggie asked. We all looked at her. "Will we spend the entire night searching? What if we don't find them all? Will we take a break? Or what if we get them all in the next two hours?"

Abbie snapped her fingers and the stones glowed green. "All right, now send your magic and your intention to the stones. Help for help, and I'm done for when you're tired or you got a dozen creatures. Otherwise, I plan on going until I get them all."

"Sounds good," Lacey said.

"Can we go now?" Maggie asked.

Abbie nodded. As they left, she said, "Levi, you know where the armory is. Take Ariella there, please." She turned to me. "You can choose any weapon in there."

"Thanks," I said.

She nodded again and left the room.

Then it was Levi and me.

He watched me, his eyes intense. "How do I convince you to go to your bedroom?"

"I think you know me better than that."

He groaned. "Come on."

I followed him out of the dining room, down the hallway, and through several turns. All the while, Levi stopped at every corner as if the creatures would be waiting on the other side.

I would probably have done the same thing if I was the one leading this party.

We entered a smaller hallway—small compared to the others, because it was still wider and taller than any residential hallway I had ever seen—and he stopped at the second door to the left. Beside it was a keypad. He entered some numbers and the door slid open.

Frowning, I watched as he entered the room and wondered how exactly that battle had gone that the witches had given him the pin number of the secure rooms in their house.

I stepped inside, intent on questioning him, but cut short when I looked around at the large room filled with weapons. Swords, daggers, throwing stars, bows and arrows, bo staffs, handguns, rifles, and even grenades.

"Wow," I whispered.

"I know. Too much for those witches."

Which brought me back to my question. "You tricked them too, right? You tried, at least. You fought your father, not because it was the noble thing to do, but because you wanted the Scarlet Hex Blade for yourself."

His jaw ticked. "I don't have to explain myself to you."

"Because I'm right." Half of my brain told me to stop talking, to go through the motions and get this night over with, but the other half couldn't contain itself. The latter won. "And they think you're this angelic demon, who came to their rescue."

He groaned. "No, I didn't come for the dagger. I didn't even know about the dagger until then, sweetheart. But I did come for something else. And Abbie knows why. She gave it to me after I saved them."

I stared at him incredulously. So, he had had an ulterior motive. "What did you get?"

He clenched his jaw and I thought he wouldn't answer. "I knew they had the Book of Wishes. I thought that if I could get to the book, I could wish my parents dead. Abbie let me use the book after the battle. I made my wish." I sucked in a breath. "But it backfired. The book doesn't deal with death, so it punished me. It bound itself to me, making me a wish-granting demon."

"That's how ..."

He nodded. "When someone makes a wish and I close my eyes, I'm communicating with the book. It sends me whatever the wisher wants, or if it can't give it to me right away, it shows me the way to get it."

"The book showed you where my wings were."

"The spell around your wings was too great. The book couldn't get it. So, it showed me their location."

I let that sink in for a little. He had come with an ulterior motive, but he had helped the witches, and when he went for his reward, he had been punished.

"It sounds like you don't like being a wish-granting demon."

"Do you think it's nice to have stupid supernaturals ask stupid things of you, sweetheart?"

I got it. I wouldn't like that either. "And the price? Is that you, or the book?"

"The book always has a price."

"You asked me for my soul. Did the book ask for it? What would the book want with my soul?"

"What is this? An interrogation?"

"Just answer the question!"

Levi worked his jaw. "The book had requested a drop of your blood. The soul was me playing with you." I stared at him, eyes wide. "Because I knew you would refuse. Remember, I had a plan?"

"Oh, I remember." And I was so done with this conversation. No matter what he did, his actions were laced with bad intentions.

I walked up to the wall displaying dozens of swords and picked up one that seemed the size of my old Celestial Blade, though it definitely weighed more.

It was okay, though. I could fight like this.

I headed to the door. "You don't need to babysit me. I can go by myself."

"And get lost in this place?" He followed me out and when I didn't stop, he dashed forward and stepped in my way, making me stop. "Stop being childish."

I flinched. "I'm not being—!"

He gave me a look and I shut my mouth. Perhaps I was

being childish, but I was being childish because he irritated me in a way nothing else had ever done before.

No, I was better than this. I was a freaking angel!

I inhaled deeply and nodded. "All right. Lead the way."

With a smug twist of his lips, Levi continued down the hallway, and it was all I could do not to kick his ass and curse his existence.

No, Ariella, think happy thoughts! Forget about the trickster demon in front of you.

It was hard to forget about him when he covered my entire sight with his tall frame and wide shoulders. A perfect frame that I had seen naked, that I had touched, and relished.

By the light, had it gotten hot in here?

Levi groaned.

What was his problem?

I shook my head, pushing those thoughts away. Now was not the time to think about that. Even though it had been a delicious night. Damn, I hadn't really allowed myself to think about that night, but now, with the subject of the story right in front of me, it was hard not to.

It had been sex, but it had been so, so good. I hadn't had a lot of experience before, but I was sure Levi's performance could be considered one of the best, if there was a rank for such a thing.

It was a shame we hated each other; otherwise, we could repeat the—

Levi spun suddenly, and I almost bumped into him. He loomed over me, glowering. "Sweetheart, can you ..." His words faded and he looked over my shoulder, his eyes going wide for half a second, then narrowing. "Turn very slowly," he whispered.

Oh, shit. I turned on my heels, slowly like Levi had asked, and inhaled deeply when I saw a handful of glowing eyes in the darkness of the hallway behind us.

"What are they?" I asked, just as low.

"Imps."

The candles along the hallway flickered on, their light dim as if to not startle the little demons, but enough for us to see there were more than a handful, all of them along the walls, watching us with curious, hungry eyes.

They were all waist height, gray-skinned, with bared pointy teeth, and huge yellow catlike eyes.

I held tighter to the sword's hilt, and beside me Levi called his darkfire.

Together, the little imps let out a skin-crawling snarl and hopped toward us on their large feet.

Levi let out several darkfire bolts, and I swung my sword. The weight felt strange in my hands, but after a few strikes, I got used to it. The imps were easy to kill, but there were too many, and when we got one down, two skipped to us in its place.

"We can't kill them all," Levi said, as he started aiming at the imps' legs and arms, to injure them instead of killing.

"Easier said than done." I groaned as three came at me at the same time. I spun out of range of one, swung my sword upward, slashing the side of another, and kicked the third one in the head, making it crash into the wall.

The vines knotted along the walls reached out and wrapped around it, keeping it in place.

"Thanks," I said to the vines, amused. One, that was so cool. Two, why didn't the hall do that with all of them?

Before I could dwell on that question, another imp

jumped on my back and bit my injured shoulder. I screamed, reached up, picked the damn thing by its pointy ears, and threw it at the wall.

Once more, the vines enveloped the creature.

Groaning, I switched my sword to my left hand. Thank goodness I had been trained in both, but of course, one was always better than the other, and it wasn't my left side.

"Are you okay, sweetheart?" Levi asked. He had created a pen of shadows and was corralling the imps inside, while still fending off the ones that escaped him.

"Just ..." I touched my shoulder and my fingertips came back bloody. "Shit."

He glanced at me. "What is it?"

Was that worry in his voice? Nah, I was too wound up to hear or think clearly.

I tried maiming the next imp who came for me, but the little thing moved fast, and I ended up stabbing him through the chest instead of slicing his side, as I first planned.

Damn it.

A sudden force on my back made me fall to my knees and lose the grip on my sword. I twisted and slapped one of the three imps that had jumped on my back before he took a bite out of my chin. Then a fourth one appeared, a bigger one, at least a head taller than the others, and a lot stronger.

It stepped on my belly, taking my breath away.

I jerked, got rid of one imp, but the other two held my arms to the sides, while the bigger one sat on my stomach, as if this was a show. I reached for my sword, but it was just out of reach.

With a scream, I was able to fling my arm hard enough to jostle the imp holding it and stretch my arm a little more. I touched the sword, closed my hand around the hilt, and brought it down on the closest imp. I immediately swung to the other one and slashed it in half. Then I aimed at the bigger one—

A darkfire bolt hit the demon square in the chest and it flew back several yards.

I sat up and glared at Levi. "I had it!"

"Of course you did, sweetheart." He moved his hands and shadows wrapped around the bigger imp, lifting it up and holding it in place.

Levi got the mirror from his pocket and pointed first at that bigger imp. It was sucked into the mirror in less than three seconds. Then he turned the mirror to the eight imps he had corralled and sucked them in too.

I pushed to my feet, wobbled, and placed a hand on the wall vines to steady myself.

When all the creatures were gone, Levi pocketed the mirror and faced me. His eyes narrowed. "When will you *not* get hurt, sweetheart?"

"When I have my magic back," I snapped.

He looked me up and down. "Ready for more?"

No, I wasn't. I was tired, breathing hard, the wound was shallow but throbbed, the sword was the wrong one for me, and I was upset about all of this. If only I had my damn magic …

But I wouldn't stop, not now.

I inhaled deeply to steady my racing heart, stood taller, and nodded. "Ready."

6

———

LEVI AND I WORKED FOR HOURS LAST NIGHT, AND WE CAPTURED another harpy, a kitsune, and three ghouls, and we killed some of them. I had gotten another slash to my upper arm, and a graze of teeth on my back, all of which Lacey had healed in the early hours of the morning.

"Did we catch them all?" I asked, praying the answer was yes.

"No," Abbie said. "We're still missing two ghouls, but they are nocturnal and won't come out of hiding until this evening. We should go rest now."

Levi handed the mirror to Abbie, who went to put the creatures back into their prisons with Maggie's help.

As Levi walked me back to my bedroom, I asked, "Why do they keep these creatures here? Aren't they better dead, or maybe in the underworld?" Or any other more specialized place.

I didn't think he would answer me, until finally, he spoke. "Two reasons. The Great Eternity Hall is one of the most secure places in the entire world, and because knowledge about each species needs to be recorded. That is done by capturing and studying them."

I understood the first one, but the second rubbed me wrong. These creatures could be single-minded evil beings, but they weren't lab rats. I didn't like knowing they were rotting away in a cell, being studied, but that was probably my righteous side trying to come out.

Levi showed me to my door but didn't wait until I got in to leave. Not that I cared.

I was so tired, I had to force myself to take a shower before falling on the bed and sleeping.

I woke up with a start, dreaming that a harpy was over me in bed, and it took me a couple of minutes to realize I was safe in my room, by myself, and hell, it was already early afternoon.

Shoot.

It wasn't as if I had any appointment, but now with most of the creatures captured (or killed), the witches would probably be able to help me and I was eager to figure out how to get my magic back.

I washed my face, brushed my teeth and my long hair, and got dressed in black leggings, a dark gray sweater, and high-heeled boots. This time, I got lost on the way to the dining room, but I found my way again. I thought I would be the only one here, but Magnus sat at the head of the table, reading a newspaper and drinking what looked like white wine.

"Good afternoon," I said, approaching the table.

He glanced at me from over the newspaper, and this time,

without any other distraction, I paid attention to him. He wasn't an ugly man, per se, but there wasn't anything attractive about him either. He had similar features to the girls, but they seemed wrong on him. The delicate nose, the long eyebrows, the full brown hair, and he wore a thin mustache and sideburns, which gave him a creepy vibe.

He wore a suit that seemed out of a fantasy movie and had an unlit pipe beside his glass.

"Afternoon," he said, sounding bored. He hid behind the newspaper again.

I halted behind the chair I had sat in last night, kind of hoping the same magic would be active right now. But my heart sank when the table remained bare.

I was about to turn when it poofed into existence: a placemat, a plate, a warm panini half wrapped in cream paper, and a glass of water. With a smile, I sat down and picked up the panini—shredded chicken in a pesto creamy sauce. The delicious smell alone made my mouth water.

I took a big bite and had to stifle a moan.

I had eaten one fourth of my panini when I noticed the uncle was looking at me. I did a double take and narrowed my eyes. "Something wrong?"

"Nothing wrong, not with me." He folded the newspaper. "But I heard there's a lot wrong with you."

Ouch. I flinched at his tone. "Well, I'm here to get help. Isn't that what the Great Eternity Hall is for?"

"If you say so." He drank half of his wine, his eyes always on mine.

Could the guy stop staring at me? I wanted to eat in peace.

"Uncle!" Trent yelled as he ran into the room.

I sighed in relief when Magnus turned to his nephew. "What are you up to, Trent?" his voice softened a little.

Trent slowed down, stopped, and ran out of the room again. A couple of seconds later, he came back inside, holding his grandma's hand.

"Good afternoon, Ariella," Belinda said to me, even though I was quiet as a mouse. "Slept well?"

I rose from the chair and turned her way. "I did, thanks for asking. How about yourself?"

She let out a chuckle. "I barely sleep anymore, dear, but I'm well rested." By now, Magnus had already made his way to her and right before he reached her, Belinda lifted her hand, as if she knew he was there. "Magnus, I need some help in my sitting room."

"I wanted to help, but Grandma says I'm too young."

She smiled. "Well, with Magnus's supervision, you might be able to."

He squealed in delight.

A faint smile adorned Magnus's lip. "Lead the way, young man."

I frowned, watching them go. Magnus had been so stand-offish with me, but with his nephew and Belinda, he had been gentle and caring.

Maybe he was not fond of visitors and strangers.

Alone and in peace, I finished my delicious panini and drank some of my water. "Thank you, Myg," I said, though I wasn't even sure if this was her magic or the hall's.

The moment I stood, the plate, the placemat, and every-thing disappeared. Seriously, if one day I settled down and had my own house, I wanted it to be magical like this, even if it was a cabin in the woods. Food that just poofed into existence and then dirty plates that disappeared forever? I was so in.

From the dining room to the library, I didn't get lost, which was a small miracle. In the library, Abbie, Maggie, and Lacey were hunched over books on the long tables behind the tree, the snake wrapped around the chair's arm. Gwen and Britt were in an alcove on the third floor's landing, with books in their hands, talking to each other. The cat was napping beside them, and the raven was perched high up, close to the ceiling.

"They are studying," Abbie said. Today she wore a dark blue gown that made her blue eyes pop.

"Magic?"

She nodded. "We have lessons almost every morning, and some afternoons."

I frowned. "Are you in the middle of a lesson? Should I come back later?"

"No, you're fine. I gave them an extra lesson to keep them distracted."

The snake moved, which made me think of another animal. "How is Rune doing?"

"He's resting in Trent's room," Maggie answered. "He's a little scared to be out until we catch the last two ghouls, but he's all right.

"I'm glad he's better."

Lacey got up and walked to me. She reached for my shoulder and my arms. "And how are you? All healed up?"

I had a scar where the vampire's stake had cut through prior to coming here, but other than that ... "I'm fine. All healed up and rested."

She smiled at me. "Glad to know I'm good at my job."

I almost smiled at her, but then I remembered something else. "About the ghouls, are we going hunting tonight too?"

"If Levi doesn't find them first," Abbie said.

"Levi?" I asked.

"That stubborn demon went to hunt for them," Lacey said. "They are probably hiding, but he said that if he found them now, while they were sleeping, it would be easier to kill them."

A pang cut through my chest at the thought of Levi infiltrating a nest and instead of finding two ghouls, he encountered twenty.

I pushed those thoughts away. What did I care about what he did or didn't do?

Abbie gestured to the table. "Are you ready to start?"

"Of course," I said, taking their lead and sitting down on a chair beside them along the table.

"All right, I know this won't be easy, but tell us everything you can about your magic, and how you lost it," Abbie asked.

I nodded and told them all about it, or at least, all I remembered.

Paimon, a former prince of the underworld, was able to absorb other supernaturals' powers, and during a battle where Paimon was trying to absorb a dragon's magic about six months ago, he absorbed mine.

"Paimon took your magic right before taking the dragon's?" Maggie asked, frowning. She was listening attentively, but Abbie was taking lots of notes.

I nodded. "That's what I heard. I passed out after my magic was gone. But Paimon didn't get all the dragon's magic. It was split between his daughter and him."

"All right, and what happened after that?" Abbie asked.

I left. Like a coward. I sat up straighter. "I heard Raika, his daughter, was able to absorb his magic, and she got the dragon's powers ... and everyone else's he had absorbed before that."

"So, Raika has all this power?" Lacey asked.

I shrugged. "I don't know. When she had only half of it, the dragon magic proved too much for her. I can't imagine she survived after taking it all."

I thought about calling, to know what had happened to her. Hopefully, they found a way to help her and she was still alive.

"Is there a way for you to call them and find out what happened?" Abbie asked. "Maybe they discovered something that will help us."

I hesitated. "Phones don't work in here, right?"

"Oh, they work in here," Maggie. "In the library."

I fished my phone from my pocket and checked. Sure enough, it had signal. "How?"

"Magic! But it's only inside the library. It doesn't work anywhere else."

"Hm ... I could call them," I said, though that would open a line I wasn't sure I was ready to deal with.

"You don't need to do that right now," Abbey said, probably sensing my hesitation.

"I say we start by gathering all the books about magic absorption and transference," Lacey suggested.

"And all the books about dragons," Maggie said. "Dragons are the most powerful supernaturals that walked this Earth, or any other known universe. They might have abilities that we haven't heard about before."

"That is a long list," Abbie said. She grabbed a huge

leather book from the corner of the table and opened it right in the middle. The book was empty. "Show me all the books, manuscripts, and scrolls about magic absorption and transference."

The pages shimmered and words appeared on the large pages. Lots and lots of words that didn't fit on those two pages but went on for several more.

I gawked at the book and once more I was amazed at how cool magic could be.

"That's a lot of books," Lacey said, her tone dejected.

"And that's just one topic," Abbie said. "I bet the list will be even longer when we get to dragons." She reached into the book and her hand disappeared inside it! Then, she pulled out four pieces of paper and distributed them to us, one for each.

"What's is this?" I glanced at the long paper in my hands and started reading the tiny words.

"A list of titles and authors, if applicable, also shelf number and placement," she explained. "Let's get to work."

Two hours later, we had the table full of books about magic absorption and transference, and we weren't done yet. At some point, Abbie stopped gathering books and stayed at the table to start skimming through them and selecting, so we wouldn't have hundreds of books to deal with once we got them all.

We hadn't even started on the dragon books yet.

It was tedious work, but the library kept impressing me.

Since first stepping foot inside, I could see this place was huge, but once I started weaving through the bookshelves, I realized it was much bigger than I first thought. The shelves went on forever and ever, and if it weren't for the labels at the beginning of each shelf, I would have gotten lost, just like I had with the rest of this place.

Following the numbers, I went to shelf 839 in the depths of the library. The farther we went, the less light came from the dome and the glass window, and we relied only on the few sconces and magical candles at the end of each long bookshelf.

Twice so far, I had been in the middle of a bookshelf, barely seeing anything—if I had had my light magic, that wouldn't be a problem—when the nearest candle shone brighter, illuminating the numbers etched on the shelf under the books. When I still couldn't find it, the book jutted out, as if someone stood on the other side and pushed it forward for me.

The first time, I was startled. The second, I thanked the hall's magic.

If only this happened every time I went for books, maybe it wouldn't take this long.

As I turned a dark corner into shelf 838, I had an idea. Maybe Abbie could cast a spell to call the books on the list. They would fly off the shelves to the table.

Hm, if there was such a spell, I was sure she would have used it already instead of having us coming and going for hours now.

I finally got to shelf 839, a dark corner of the library. I almost reached for the candle stationed between shelves, but

I was sure it would brighten if it got too dark and I couldn't read the numbers or the book titles.

As I made my way to the middle of the endless shelf, it got darker and darker. I frowned. Was the candle playing with me now? It had helped me before. Was there such a thing as a tired magical candle?

I started looking around the books to see if I was in the right section or needed to go farther down the shelf, but the light got even darker.

"Hey!" I called out. "Can't you help me now?" Nothing happened. "Please?" The candle flickered twice, almost going out. "What the hell?"

I turned toward the beginning of the bookshelf, to grab the damn candle from its sconce.

It went out.

I froze as I was plunged into darkness.

My heart beat fast, a reaction to the surprise. If I didn't know better, I would think this was Levi pulling a prank on me. But he wasn't this petty.

I blinked twice, adjusting my vision to the darkness, trying to see the end of the bookshelf.

Instead, I saw a dark figure crouched right in front of me.

I screamed, my heart rate picking back up.

The ghoul leapt for me and I ran in the opposite direction.

Just to see the other ghoul above my head, holding on to the bookshelf.

My next scream lodged in my throat, and for a moment, I could barely breath, much less move.

Slowly, the ghouls came closer and I took a look at them. They seemed like a mix of skeleton and zombies, with grayish muscle-like skin, white eyes, no hair, pointed ears, razor-sharp teeth, and long claws on their hands and feet. When they stood, their backs were hunched, but they were still taller than me.

Then they hissed and I woke up from the daze.

The one on the top lunged and I ducked under it and ran.

The shelves all looked the same, and I couldn't slow down to check the numbers. For all I knew, I was going deeper into the library, instead of heading to my friends.

I didn't dare look back to check on the creatures, but I could hear them. The ghouls were fast and they were gaining on me.

Out of breath, I clambered away from them, holding on to the shelves to keep me upright. I yelped when a book flew off the shelf right in front of me and landed at my feet, wide open. A soft glow came from the pages, and for half a second, I wondered what the hell was going on. But something in me propelled me forward. I crouched down, touched the glow, and pulled out a long, silver sword.

I didn't have time to think about it.

The ghouls screeched and I turned, the sword pointed at their chests. Not expecting a weapon, one of them ran toward me and right into the blade. With the momentum, both of us went down, and I landed hard on my back and head. The creature snapped its teeth at me a handful of times, but the hilt of the sword, which I was still holding tight, kept it distant enough.

Then the creature's dark eyes widened and it went still. The sword disappeared and the creature's heavy weight fell over me.

I turned my face and groaned in agony.

Then the second ghoul loomed over me, hunger in his depthless eyes, in the snap of his teeth.

Suddenly, a dark bolt crashed into the ghoul, sending it far from me to the darkness between the shelves, where I couldn't see it.

Inhaling deeply, I gathered my strength to push the creature's body away, or at least lift it for long enough so I could slip from underneath.

Then someone pushed the body and it rolled to the side.

By the light, what had happened?

Breathing hard, I pushed to my elbows as Levi crouched beside me. "Are you okay, sweetheart?"

The candles at the shelves' ends came back to life, but kept their lights dim. It was enough for me to see something deep and dangerous in his blue eyes.

"I'm ..." I pushed to my feet and scoffed. "This is ridiculous. I'm a monster magnet."

"Sweetheart, are you hurt?"

Why did this keep happening to me? I was always the damsel in distress. At least this time, I had been able to deal with the monsters myself. The result: one freaking irritated and tired angel.

"Light, how I miss my magic."

Levi stepped right to me, his giant figure looming over me. "Sweetheart, talk to me."

"What do you want me to say? Why was I the only one attacked? It's like these creatures know I'm vulnerable. They wait for me in the shadows, literally."

Levi grabbed my shoulders. "Ariella, are you hurt?" He looked me up and down, as if expecting I was broken.

"See, even you know I'm breakable now."

"Do you need me to take you to the infirmary?" he pressed, ignoring my comments. "Or maybe to Lacey?"

I slapped his hands away and took a large step back. "What the hell do you care?"

With a growl, Levi pushed into me and turned me around, caging me in against the bookshelf. With one hand, he cupped my jaw and neck, almost too tight, and the other he closed around my waist. He pushed his leg between mine, his thick thigh rubbing at a sensitive place.

He leaned his head toward mine. "I care, sweetheart," he whispered, his mouth right at my ear. His breath washed over my neck, making me shiver. "I care more than I want to. I can't get you off my mind, and every time I close my eyes, I see you spread out on that table, writhing in pleasure and moaning for me." His hand slid down from my waist to my ass, pushing me harder against him.

A half moan escaped my lips and it was all I could do not to grind my hips against his legs. I bet he could get me off just by whispering obscene stuff and rubbing me like this.

"I want you more than I have ever wanted anything in my life, and it has been torture to stay away from you." He dragged his lips across my jaw and I shivered. "But I try, because I don't know if this is really us, or if it's the bond. And—"

It was like a bucket of icy water.

I shoved my hands hard against his chest and he took a step back. Without his leg holding me, I almost fell forward, but was able to gracefully steady myself.

That didn't stop me from glaring at him with all my might. "What the hell did you say?"

"Well, I thought I was about to make you come—"

"About the bond!" I almost shouted. "What do you mean the bond? We broke it. Your sister helped me. The bond is gone." Levi averted his eyes. Oh, no. "Tell me the bond is gone."

His gaze found mine again, hard and intense. "The bond didn't break, it changed."

7

———————

I MARCHED AWAY FROM HIM AND BACK TO THE LONG TABLES, checking the shelf numbers to make sure I was going the right way. I could hear his footsteps behind me, but I was sure that if I turned to tell him to stop following him, I would punch him.

I knew where punching him had led before.

Abbie was hunched over several books and Lacey had come out of the shelves, carrying more books. Thankfully, Maggie, Gwen, and Britt were nowhere to be seen.

I stopped across the table from them, my head barely above the tall pile of books, crossed my arms, and asked, "Is there a bond connecting us? Levi and me, I mean?"

Lacey almost dropped the books and stared at Levi with huge eyes.

Abbie frowned. "Yes. Why?"

"But we broke it." I stared at Lacey. "You and I broke the bond three weeks ago."

"About that," she said sheepishly.

"What?" I almost barked.

"Remember when you fell into the circle during the ritual?" Lacey asked. If she could, she would hide under the table.

Of course, I remembered. "I asked you if that had messed up anything."

"I thought it didn't," she said. Her gaze shifted to Levi, who was standing a couple of feet behind me. "But it did."

I whirled to him. "You lied to me."

He shrugged. "I thought it was what you wanted to hear."

Once more, he had lied to me. Tricked me yet again. I shook my head, not knowing where to start. "So what now? Do you still feel pain when you are away from me? Do you feel my feelings?"

His brows slammed down. "I ... it doesn't hurt as much anymore, but I do feel a deep tug that can get quite painful when you're away, and your feelings are muted. I have to pay attention to them to feel them."

"What else?" I asked, sure there was more.

"Don't you feel it too?" Abbie asked.

I glanced at her. "Feel what?"

"The bond," she said. "I can see the thread. It's both ways. Yours is a lot fainter, but it's definitely there."

Eyes round, I placed a hand on my chest and opened my mouth to deny it, but then closed it again. I had felt several tugs and pulls, sometimes even painful, when I thought about him or saw him.

"Oh, shit," I muttered. "This can't be happening."

"I'm sorry it didn't work," Lacey said. "We can try again and—"

"We should," I snapped. "Or we can find a better ritual, one that we can't mess up." I looked up at the millions of books and countless pieces of knowledge this place held. "There has to be a spell that can do that."

"Well, we can pause looking for a way to give you back your magic so we can break the bond between the two of you," Abbie said, sounding a little annoyed. "What do you prefer?"

Ouch.

I felt like screaming, running, punching, crying. This wasn't how any of this was supposed to go, damn it.

"I ... I need a break," I muttered, walking away from them.

"Don't get lost," Abbie called out. "It'll be dark again and we still have two ghouls loose."

"No, we don't," I said back, without turning.

I heard their voices as Levi told them what happened, and then I exited the library.

I kept walking, down the hallways and into places I had no idea were in here. A music room, a theater room, a small ballroom, a conference room, several small reading nooks, and dozens of galleries. I walked by another archway adorned by vines, and at first it looked like the other hundred I had seen, but the light coming from this one was brighter, yellower. I stopped before the archway and the vines moved, twisting until a white flower showed beside me.

With a small smile, I touched the flower and it fell in my hand. "Thank you." I took the flower to my nose and inhaled deeply. The sweet, earthy scent brought me a sense of calm.

I walked past the archway and found myself in a large courtyard. Stone paths were flanked by low bushes and white and yellow flowers. I took one of the stone paths toward the center, where a circle and wooden chairs were. In the middle was a round pit in the ground and some firewood. A fire pit? Now I wanted a s'more.

Holding the flower, I sat on one of the chairs and leaned back. I glanced up, toward the beautiful blue sky and tried opening my mind, clearing my thoughts and just being.

Easier said than done.

I was a freaking fallen angel without her magic and her Celestial Sword, who was still bonded to an evil higher demon who kept tricking me.

I couldn't even think of what else I was missing, what else I didn't know, what Rhodes was doing right now, and everything in between.

There was nothing I could do from here, and the more I thought about it, the more desperate I became.

I felt lost, useless.

Before, I had a purpose. I had gone to the academy and joined the ranks of guardians to protect humankind from evil.

That was my whole life.

But since that fateful day, that failed mission, what was my goal? My purpose?

To find my wings? Check. To get my magic back? Working on it. How about my sword? Not sure that one was recoverable.

And then what? What could I do? And what if I had it all wrong? What if I had misread Rhodes's intentions, his plans? What if he was trying to save Elysium from a terrible fate? What if he was as evil as the worst demon and had corrupted Adona?

What was I supposed to do about that? How could I save us all?

I groaned, frustrated with my active mind as it took off and ran from me again.

Why did I keep imagining crazy scenarios when I knew nothing of what was going on up there, other than me being accused of killing my friends?

Until I knew, I shouldn't assume.

I had to focus on one step at a time. And the next step was clearly recovering my magic, not breaking a forsaken bond.

From the way Levi acted when we were alone between the bookshelves, the bond was affecting him more than he let on, but he would survive. He was a grown demon and could endure a few more days tied to me, right?

Right.

My magic came first. Always.

I closed my eyes and tried to remember the feeling of magic in my veins, of holding a bolt of light in my hands, of feeling so pure and powerful, it was electric. I held on to that. I had to hold on to that. This feeling was what was going to get me through.

I let out a long breath, finally more centered than before.

I had a damn mission and nothing would stop me from finishing it.

"Ariella?" I opened my eyes and looked to the side. Maggie stood there, her green eyes full of light. "Are you okay?"

"Yes. I was focusing, remembering what's important." I inhaled in and out again, another cleansing breath. "Why? Anything wrong?"

"Abbie sent me to check on you," she said.

"Sorry."

She shrugged. "Don't be. I was about to play babysitter with Trent, but now Gwen has to go."

I smiled. "Is taking care of him so bad?"

"It's not bad, but it can be boring."

I nodded. "How old are you?"

"Nineteen."

Angels lived differently from humans, but at nineteen, I was at the academy and living my best life. Sneaking out at night to do things we shouldn't, making friends and enemies, falling in love and having my heart broken.

"Did you ever leave the Grand Eternity Hall?" I asked.

She nodded. "With my parents, before they died. Once every couple of months, they liked to take us out to see the world, to know what was happening out there, and how technology was advancing."

"Did you like those outings?"

"Oh, yeah. We've been to New York City, Los Angeles, Rome, London, Sydney, Hong Kong ... but my favorite was Paris."

I felt a little jealous of her. I was almost four years her senior and I hadn't left North America.

"It sounds like they were great parents."

"The best," Maggie said, her voice soft. She smiled at me, a sad line on her pink lips. Then her eyes glossed over and she went rigid. "Ariella." Her voice turned eerie. "Your heart will be ripped from your chest, taken to the black abyss, the trip there might claim your life, but to survive what's coming, you'll need it."

She blinked and her eyes went back to normal.

I gawked at her. "What was that?"

"Oh no, what did I say?"

"Something about my heart being ripped from my chest and that I'll need it to survive." Who wouldn't?

"That was a vision-slash-prophecy. Sorry, I can't tell the difference between them yet."

"Do your visions-slash-prophecies always come true?" I asked, trying to decipher her ominous words.

She shook her head. "From what my mother told me, our visions are more like possibilities of the future, the most likely to happen if you don't change anything affecting it at this moment. But if you change something, then the vision is null."

So, when I figured out what she meant, if it was bad, all I had to do was change something affecting it? That sounded simple enough.

But how would I stop my heart from being ripped from me? That didn't make sense. If that happened, I would be dead!

"Sorry I'm not much help," she continued. "Abbie is a great teacher, but she was also learning when our parents died, and she doesn't know much about my gift." She let out a long breath. "I would probably know if it was a vision or a prophecy if my mother was still here."

I pushed that vision-slash-prophecy out of my head. I had enough on my plate as it was. I wouldn't add ominous and uncertain things to it.

Instead, I reached to the side and patted Maggie's hand. "I'm sorry you lost your parents so young." I knew the feeling. I had lost my father when I was at the academy, and in some way, I had lost my mother and my sister five years ago.

She offered me a small smile. "We should go back. We have many books to look through."

I nodded. "Right."

This time, following Maggie, it was a straight shot to the library and we were back there in less than five minutes. I swear, this hall either didn't like me much, or it liked me enough to feel comfortable playing with me.

In the library, the scene hadn't changed. Abbie was kneeling on a chair, looking over five open books over the table, with more piled high around her. Lacey was on the other side of the table, sorting books, and Gwen was helping for a change, checking the list each of us received.

I glanced around, expecting to see Levi helping.

Lacey looked at me. "He's not here."

I shrugged. "I didn't ask anything."

"But I can see it in your eyes," she said, sounding almost mad.

"All right, where did he go, then?" I should find him and tell him that unfortunately my magic was more important than this crazy bond, but we would break it soon.

I promised.

Again.

"He's not here," she repeated. "He got a call and had to leave."

Oh, he wasn't here, as not in this room, but not in the entire Grand Eternity Hall.

My heart sank at the thought, a little pain snaked through my chest, and I told myself that was this damned bond.

Nothing else.

8

For the next two days, I spent most of my time in the library along with Abbie, Maggie, and Lacey, researching magic absorption.

Abbie was in charge of skimming through the books and selecting the ones we should look into, and Maggie was the one reading the selected ones making sure to leave bookmarks on any passage of interest, while Lacey and I set aside the discarded ones, and brought more books to the table.

This morning, we finally started gathering the books about dragons.

At this rate, I would recover my magic next year, which was much better than never, so I didn't complain.

In the mornings, Abbie gave lessons to Gwen, Britt, and Trent, and later in the day, she checked on those. In the afternoon, Gwen and Britt sometimes showed up and wanted to help, but Trent spent most of his time with their grandmother.

I had had lunch and dinner with the family a handful of times now, and Magnus continued to puzzle me. He looked at me and Lacey as if we were bugs, but he was kind to his family—most of the time. Sometimes, he complained they were too loud, or too happy, or should change the subject.

So far, I had deduced Magnus was a sensitive warlock.

At night, I stayed in the library and researched about bonds and ways to break them. But I thought the library, or the entire hall, was still playing with me. Abbie had given me a brief list of books about bonds, saying that was enough to get me started, and every time I went to look for a book, I found the half inch to one inch space between other books where it should have been, but there was nothing.

No books.

Once, I asked Maggie about it. She got the list from me and retrieved three books in minutes. "They were all there," she said. She set down the books on the table and turned back to her task.

I thanked her but when I went to grab the books, they were gone.

"I think the hall is telling you to focus on one thing at a time," Lacey said.

It seemed that way, though that irritated me even more. Why couldn't I do both? I was focusing on the most important thing: I spent nine to ten hours of my day researching my magic, and one on the bond. Wasn't that enough?

I grabbed four other books about dragons from the shelves and stopped by one that supposedly explained the difference between bonds, how they came to be, and if they were breakable or not.

As usual, the book was missing.

With a sigh, I walked to the tables and dropped the heavy

books. I sat down beside Maggie as she slid her fingers across the page and picked up a bookmark.

"Something interesting?" I asked.

She nodded, placed the bookmark in the book, and put it on the to-be-studied-later pile. "This book says there are distinct kinds of magic absorption. It can be partial or full, and it also differs according to the type of supernaturals. I'm not sure it'll explain what happens when a higher demon takes magic from an angel, but there's only one way to know."

I knew what happened. The angel became human, weak and useless in her world.

A phone dinged and Lacey grabbed her cell from her pocket. She looked at the screen, then at me, then typed something.

"What is it?" I asked, already annoyed.

"Nothing." She tucked her phone away.

"Lacey, was that Levi?"

"Yes." She pouted. "He was just checking in."

"Asking if I'm all right." Of course, he wanted me to be all right. If I wasn't, he would hurt, literally. She nodded. Damn, I would have to have a conversation about boundaries with him. "When is he coming back?"

"He doesn't know," she said. "He went out to—" Lacey pressed her lips tight, which made me think of the worst.

"Torture an innocent soul? Take advantage of weak supernaturals? Steal the candy of children?"

"Ariella," she said with a sigh.

"What? Just because he did one or two good things in his entire life, doesn't mean he isn't evil."

"It's the opposite." Lacey's voice turned sour. "Just because he did a couple" —I raised my eyebrows— "all right, several bad things, doesn't mean he's evil."

"You know the phrase innocent until proven guilty? I prefer guilty until proven innocent with him. And so far, he hasn't wanted to prove his innocence."

"Ariella." Abbie looked up from the books spread before her. "Can we drop this subject?"

Shit, I had been so worked up, I had offended my host. "Sorry, I can't seem to let it go."

"I—"

"You have a visitor."

I almost jumped out of my chair when Myg's voice echoed through the library.

"Are we expecting anyone?" Maggie asked.

Abbie shook her head. "It might be one of our regular clients." She gestured to Myg. "Bring him in."

Myg walked around the large tree, and in ten seconds, walked back with three figures behind her—an old witch and two males, though I had no idea what they were.

"Mrs. Dennis." Abbie stood and smiled at the witch. "It's so good to see you. How are you? And Mr. Twitches?"

"I'm fine, dear, and Mr. Twitches is energetic and spoiled as always."

Abbie's eyes hardened as she took in the other two people. "You brought friends."

"Oh, yes." Mrs. Dennis beckoned the man forward. "This is Elias and Eugene. I thought you could help them."

Abbie shifted her weight. I could see she wasn't comfortable with that. "Hi, Elias and Eugene. I'm Abigail Evermore, the owner and protector of the Grand Eternity Hall."

"I'm Elias," the oldest said. He was in his late twenties, but guessing ages was tricky with supernaturals. "And this is my brother, Eugene."

"It's nice to meet you, Abigail, " Eugene said. He had cropped hair and a short beard, and he was almost as tall as Levi, but a lot less menacing.

"How can I help you?" Abbie asked.

Elias glanced at the witch and she nodded her chin encouragingly.

He fished a bunched cloth from the pocket of his jacket. He unfolded it and showed us the beautiful necklace lying in the cloth. "This has been in my family for generations, and I believe it's cursed."

Abbie approached him. "What do you mean?"

"All the women in my family who have worn this necklace have died in childbirth." He gulped. "The latest was my wife and my son died a few days later."

My heart squeezed.

"I'm so sorry." Abbie pressed a hand to her chest. "Was your wife a lion shifter like you?"

He was a lion shifter. Interesting.

He nodded. "Her family was close to mine. But now ..."

Abbie reached for the necklace. "Do you mind if I examine it?"

He pulled back. "Don't touch it! I can't guarantee what happens if you do. I'm guessing the curse affects females who wear it but I would rather not test it."

"And what do you want us to do, then?"

"I want to get rid of it, but I can't destroy it, and I shouldn't throw it away and risk having another person finding it. That was when Mrs. Dennis told me about you. She said you have a secure safe for these kinds of objects."

"That is true." Abbie seemed intrigued.

Besides, Maggie was already moving. She retrieved a tray from under the table and went to them.

"You can put it here," Maggie said. "We promise not to touch it."

"Though, while we keep it safe, would you mind if I studied it?" Abbie asked. I could see this excited her.

"As long as you don't touch it." Elias dropped the cloth and necklace on the tray.

"I promise." She nodded at Maggie, who carried the tray to a distant corner of the long tables.

"Thank you, dear," Mrs. Dennis said. "You're as kind and helpful as usual."

"Is there anything else we can help with?" Abbie asked.

"I brought something for your grandmother." Mrs. Dennis got a small package from inside her purse. "It's her favorite candy. Would you mind if I give it to her?"

Abbie pressed her lips into a thin line. "You know what, it's almost suppertime. If you don't have any plans, why don't you all stay and dine with us? Then you can give the candy to Grandma."

Mrs. Dennis, Elias, and Eugene exchanged glances. She looked nervous but nodded and Elias smiled. "That would be our pleasure."

I leaned against the windowsill and looked out at the vast forest beyond. Once more, I wondered where we were, if the Grand Eternity Hall existed in its own realm. How was it created? By whom? Who gave the Evermores power over it?

Maybe after I got my magic back, did whatever I had to do in Elysium, and broke the bond with Levi, I could come back here and ask the girls. I bet they knew. Or they could point me to books that talked about the hall's history. I was sure there were several volumes recording everything.

I let out a sigh.

After Abbie invited Mrs. Dennis, Elias, and Eugene to stay for dinner, Myg saw them to a sitting room where they would meet Belinda, Trent, and Magnus.

"I'll be there soon," Abbie told them.

When they left, Maggie picked up the tray and let the necklace drop inside a squared glass case. "So, no one accidentally touches it," she said.

One by one, the sisters left to clean up to meet the visitors and have supper. Even Lacey went with them.

I had come back to my room to wash up, but I was in no rush. I just wanted to eat one of those wonderful, magical meals.

Now, as I wasted time doing nothing in my bedroom, my mind had to go to Levi.

Break the bond with Levi.

The bond made me think about him. It made me want him, it made me want to be kissed by him again, to have him inside of me—

I shook my head. Yes, sex with him was great, the best I had ever had, though that wasn't saying much as my experience was limited, but at some point, I had to forget about it, right? We did it, got it out of our system, and were done.

Now we could move on.

If only it were that simple.

A pang cut through my chest and I cursed under my breath.

All right, maybe it was time to go to the dining room. If it was too early for supper, I could meet everyone in the sitting room, even if I had to endure small talk with strangers.

It was better than staying here and yearning for a demon who didn't deserve my feelings, real or not.

I stopped at the closet to look at myself in the mirror— everything was normal. My leggings, my long-sleeved tee, my boots. I was even having a great hair day and my silver-blond locks fell into smooth cascades down my back.

Even though my phone only worked at the library, I stuffed it into my leggings' side pockets as I used it to check the time, set reminders, and make notes on the notes app.

Then I walked out of my bedroom, this time sure I knew the way to the dining room. I turned into two hallways, then started turning a third and skidded to a stop.

There was a wall in the way. I glanced around, confused. I was sure this was the way, but the wall seemed to continue, as if it had always been there.

Was I lost again?

I backtracked and decided to try another way.

Three turns later, the same thing happened.

"What the hell?" I looked up at the ceiling. "Are you trying to make me mad? Well, you're succeeding."

The hall didn't answer.

Huffing, I turned around and tried yet another hallway. By now, I was lost, for sure, but I knew that if I kept trying, I would soon find a staircase. Or I would bump into someone and go with them to the dining room.

Finally, after what seemed like forever, I made it downstairs and into the hallway where the sitting and the dining room were located. I was probably late for supper by now, damn it.

About ten feet from the archway, vines shot out of the knots along the walls and created a fence right before me.

"You are playing with me," I said, becoming upset. "Why are you doing this? Did I hurt you? Did I break something? Do you think I'll hurt the Evermores?"

Beyond the dining room, all the lights went off, and behind me, the lights flickered furiously.

What was the hall trying to tell me?

Tired of this game, I climbed the vines. They moved and tried wrapping around my legs, but I jumped before they could catch me.

I stepped into the dining room and the lights came back on.

I froze, my heart skipping several beats.

Everyone was sitting around the table, but they seemed dead? Fainted? Some leaned back in their chairs, their heads lolled to the side, others were bent over the table, their heads over the placemats.

I raced to the table. "Maggie?" I touched her shoulder. "Lacey?" I reached across the table and grabbed her hand.

Then I saw Abbie's chest move up and down slowly.

Asleep. They were all asleep.

But why? How?

I looked around. I saw Belinda, Trent, Abbie, Maggie, Gwen, Britt, Lacey, Mrs. Dennis, and Magnus.

Even the animals were here, in their usual corner, all sleeping.

But there were two people missing.

"Are you looking for us?"

9

ELIAS AND EUGENE STOOD IN THE DOORWAY, THEIR ARMS shifted into their lion forms.

"What's going on?" I asked, rounding the table.

They walked into the room.

"Don't you know?" Elias asked. His tone from before, the dejected mien, the sad voice ... it was all gone. "Eugene thought you were smarter than that."

I knew why they were here. To get me for the reward. That much was clear. "What did you do to them?"

"Remember that necklace?" Eugene asked. "Yeah, it was all a lie. The whole thing. We found out Mrs. Dennis had access to the Grand Eternity Hall, where we had heard the fugitive angel was hiding, so we threatened her son if she didn't help us. We got a random necklace of hers and made her enchant it with a sleeping spell that would work on witches and warlocks."

Elias laughed. "Her included."

"Don't worry," Eugene said. "Your friends will wake up tomorrow morning with a headache."

Hiding behind a tall chair, I reached into the table and got a steak knife that was there, out of place.

Elias tsked. "What do you think you'll be able to do with that?"

I raised the knife. "Kill you."

He laughed again. "You're funny."

"Maybe that's why the angels are offering such a large reward for you," Eugene said, and Elias laughed once more.

They took slow steps toward me, as if they were enjoying this game.

I wasn't.

My heart was beating out of my chest, and my hand shook around the knife.

I almost told them to stop. Right now, there was nothing I could say or do that would persuade them to change their minds.

There was only one thing left to do.

I bolted to the backdoor, where I had seen Myg going several times, but had never gone through myself.

The lights went on in the narrow corridor, and when I turned a corner, they went off, but blinked on the other side.

"All right, all right," I muttered, following the lights.

The hall hadn't played with me. It had tried to steer me away from the dining room so these two couldn't get me. Damn, I had been so stupid. I wouldn't doubt the hall ever again.

I ran through a giant, half-modern, half-ancient kitchen, through another narrow corridor, past a closet, and into a large hallway like the ones on the second floor.

The lights continued blinking, taking me away from the

dining room. Behind me, I heard Elias and Eugene on my tail, cursing as vines sprouted from the walls to stop them. But with their powerful claws, they cut through them like paper.

The lights flickered in the library. I rushed in and the doors closed on their own.

I stopped for a second to catch my breath. What now? Would the doors hold them until the others woke up? They said it would be tomorrow morning. Could I hide in here until then?

"Come out, little angel!" Eugene shouted.

The door shook with their heavy bangs.

No, it wouldn't hold until tomorrow morning.

The lights flickered beside one of the long tables. I dashed there ... and then stopped. "What are you trying to tell me?"

A vine lengthened from the big tree, wrapped around my leg, and slipped its tip inside my pocket, right where my phone was.

I gasped and grabbed my phone.

The vine retreated.

My hands shook as I unlocked my phone. I almost dropped it as a huge bang came from the door and one hinge flew out.

I opened the contact app, found his name easily, and pressed it.

The phone rang three times.

"Now is not a suitable time, sweetheart. I—"

"There are two lion shifters here," I said as fast as I could. "They sedated everyone—"

"WHAT?"

"—but me. I'm locked in the library, but the door won't hold."

I shouted as a bang louder than the previous ones echoed from the door and another hinge shot toward the tree.

"Ariella, listen to me." There was a bite to his word. "First, take a deep breath." I did as he said. "Second, go into the bookshelves, hide there. The hall will help you."

"And then what?"

"Then pray I get there before they lay a hand on you. Otherwise, I won't just kill them. I'll skin them alive, feed them to piranhas, pull them out when they are an inch from death, and rip their hearts out with my bare hands."

I shuddered. From the hard tone of his voice, I knew he was serious.

"Levi—"

The loudest bang yet made me jump. The doors went down. In their lion forms, Eugene and Elias ran at me.

I suppressed a scream and ran toward the bookshelves to my right.

The vines shot out from the tree, wrapping around one of the shifters, while a bookshelf extended across the floor until it reached the table, blocking the path of another.

I stepped between two bookshelves and stopped.

Why would I hide in the dark, when I could get out of reach another way?

I called my wings, felt the familiar course of the magic as they came forward. They ripped the back of my shirt and spread wide. I pushed with my feet, flapped them, and went up to the glass dome.

The lions jumped on the long table, walking over the books, pushing them out, ripping pages, making a huge mess.

I was away from their reach now, and safe.

Eugene transformed back into his human form, and stood several feet under me, naked. He placed a hand on his waist. "Do you think that will be enough to escape us?"

"It has worked so far." Even if so far was only a minute or two.

I could stay here and flap my wings until Levi arrived, or I could do something. I might be magicless, but I wasn't helpless. I could fight them, especially now that I had the advantage of being in the air.

Besides, I had no idea how long it would take Levi to get here, and my wings were like any other limb: it could get to a point when I couldn't fly anymore.

"Silly angel," Eugene said.

I aimed the kitchen knife at him—and realized I had dropped my phone somewhere. No time to worry about that. I threw the knife as Eugene shifted back. The blade scratched his back as he pounced off the table.

He and Elias ran to the stairs on opposite sides.

What, they thought they could get to me from the second floor?

The lions showed up on the last landing, a few feet from my wings on each side. I tucked my wings in a little, which made it harder to flap and keep myself afloat, but it was doable.

For now.

They let out a loud roar. Together, they both shifted back to their human forms. Eugene let out a laugh as he reached for a thick book from the shelf behind him. Elias broke the iron sconce from the shelf's end.

I snickered. Were they going to throw those at me? I was

fast with my wings. I could dodge their attack easily. In fact, I could do something else.

Not waiting for them to act first, I flew down, grabbed the steak knife I had thrown earlier, and flew directly toward Eugene.

I was fast and my momentum was enough to bury the knife in his chest, but when I was right in front of him, he threw the book up like a brick.

I frowned, confused, and lost a little bit of my momentum.

On the other side, Elias threw the sconce up too.

Realization hit me a second too late. I flew toward the door as the dome shattered and large pieces of glass fell on me.

I felt something tugging me back and fell to the floor like a sack of potatoes. When I lifted my head, I saw the big piece of glass stuck in the stone floor that would have cleaved me in two, and the retreating vines that had saved my life.

"Thanks," I muttered.

Hurting from the lacerations across my skin, I pushed to my feet, spread my wings, and flapped. But I cried out in pain as one of my wings bent in an odd direction, cut from the glass shards.

Shit.

Without a choice, I tucked my wings, groaned in pain, and ran to the door.

I didn't make it ten steps before a lion lunged at my back and I fell again.

I grabbed broken glass, turned around, and stabbed the lion in the shoulder.

It let out a painful roar, then bit down on my arm. I cried out.

"Don't kill her!" one of them shouted. I was too far gone with pain to pay attention. "We need her alive."

The lion retreated half a step and shifted. With the shard still stuck in his shoulder and bleeding, Eugene leaned over me and smirked. "You're done for, angel."

He reached for my middle. I grabbed another shard, but this time he was prepared. He slapped my hand away, making me drop the shard, and then punched my temple.

I saw stars.

I didn't fully faint, but I couldn't hang on to consciousness for long.

Eugene had carried me over his shoulders through a portal, into some dark place, where another supernatural waited for us, and then into the backseat of a car. My wrists and ankles were tied with non-magical rope, but even though I willed my body to move, to break the ropes, to open the car's door, and jump out, it didn't obey.

I didn't know how much time had passed, but at some point, we were on the road, and I was feeling slightly more awake.

Pretending to be still passed out, I took inventory of my surroundings. We were in a small car. I sat beside Eugene, Elias was in the passenger seat, and another man was driving.

I tried picking up what he was, but I was too weak to even try.

I had to get out of here.

Before I could fully plan this out, I lifted my bound wrists, brought them over the front seat, and strangled the driver with the ropes.

Eugene tugged at my arms, Elias turned and tried intervening, but that only tightened the ropes more. The car jerked, went off the road, fell into a ditch, and hit a thick tree.

I was thrown against the seat, hard, and my head was dizzy for a moment. No, I had to push through the haze. I had to get out of here. Trying to focus, I looked around.

The front glass was broken, mine was cracked, the driver was smashed between his seat and the wheel, dead. Elias and Eugene had their seat belts on and were having a tough time moving.

Something glittered from the car's floor.

The steak knife.

What was it doing here? I didn't question it. I took the knife and went for Eugene. He sobered up half a second before the knife plunged in the middle of his chest.

He groaned, his eyes wide.

From the front seat, Elias twisted as much as he could and shouted. "No!"

I elbowed the window by my side, finally breaking it, and crawled through. I felt the broken glass scratching my arms and legs, but it didn't matter, I needed to get out of here.

Though I tried catching myself, my body was hurt and sore, my mind addled, and I fell on the rough ground hard.

Groaning, I pushed through the pain and the haze, sat up on my knees, and grabbed a small glass shard to cut my ropes. I freed my ankles but before I could work on my wrists, I heard the sound of the car groaning as Elias exited it.

With renewed energy, I escaped from the ditch and clambered into the road.

Elias let out a roar as he ran after me. I glanced over my shoulder and panic started anew as he gained ground as a lion. He launched himself toward me. I sidestepped him, but he was fast. He hit my shoulder with his big paw and I fell on the hard ground, arm first, and pain radiated through my limb.

By the light, I must have broken it.

Elias spun and came at me. I tried gathering myself, but the lion crawled over me and pushed me to the ground. With his paws on my shoulders, he let out a loud roar right in my face, his breath foul.

I pushed my hands inside his mouth and stabbed the glass shard deep into his throat.

The lion sputtered for two seconds before falling heavy over me.

I shouted in anger, in pain, in fear. I was pinned to the ground, hurt, and alone on this dark road. Tears brimmed in my eyes and I let myself take thirty seconds to steady my heart and my breathing.

Then I pushed the lion up a little and crawled from underneath him. The ropes around my wrists were loose, and it was easy to undo them now. I rubbed at my red skin, though my wrists were what hurt the least.

I looked around.

There was nothing but a long road, trees, and darkness.

I could go back to the car, search for someone's phone, call Levi, or Hazel ... but I really didn't want to go back there. I needed to get out of here.

I called my wings, tried to spread them out, and flap

them, but one was twisted, and the other had several rips. I would never be able to fly like this.

I continued down the road, dragging my feet and doing my best not to pass out. This road was bound to lead somewhere, to some town, and when it did, I would find a store, someone who would let me make a call.

Not even ten minutes later, when I thought I would finally break and faint right here, I heard the zoom of wings, as if a big bird was soaring through the sky.

I glanced up at the darkness and saw a shape fast approaching.

My heart seized and panic threatened to spill.

No, please, not again.

But then I recognized him.

In his powerful demon form, Levi landed six feet from me. He didn't stop moving when his feet touched the ground. He ran to me, almost crashed into me, and wrapped me in his big arms.

I broke then.

I clung to him and a sob shook my body.

He held me tight, a big hand on the back of my neck, the other securely wrapped around my waist, and his temple touching mine.

"I've got you now," he whispered. "You're safe, sweetheart."

He glanced above my head and a growl started deep in his chest.

I followed his gaze, afraid another supernatural had popped out of nowhere, but I could only see Elias' body on the road.

"They are all dead," I said, my voice hoarse.

"That's my girl," Levi said, sounding proud. He hooked his arm under my knees and picked me up. "Let's get you out of here."

He pushed up and we took to the sky.

I hung on to him but didn't have the strength to keep conscious.

In seconds, I fell asleep.

10

I woke up slowly, a little dazed. I brought a hand to my eyes to cover the crack of light coming through the half-covered big window to my left.

Why was I feeling so groggy and sore?

Then it all came back to me and I tensed, my heart speeding up.

I inhaled deeply and forced my heart to calm down. I was in my bed in the Grand Eternity Hall, wearing the nightshirt I always did, with the fluffy, soft covers up to my chest.

In an armchair beside the bed, with his elbow on the chair's arm, and his fisted hand on his temple, Levi slept.

I turned to my side, tucked my hands underneath the pillow, and watched him. He probably arrived back here with me hours ago, in the middle of the night, wearing nothing but ripped pants.

But now he was crispy clean in slacks and a button-up shirt, with not two, but three buttons undone.

Even though he had been busy when I called him, he had dropped everything and come to save me.

This time, I had saved myself.

Though I was glad he had come to collect me. I had no idea how I would get back here if he hadn't.

And now here he was, watching over me as if he cared.

What had he said last night?

That's my girl.

Right. Like calling me sweetheart, that was probably what he said to all females that got too close.

Still, I couldn't help the pull inside my chest and the little sliver of pride. It had taken almost everything in me, but I had beaten three supernaturals by myself.

And they—

I sat up with a jerk. "The witches," I whispered, remembering everyone in the hall had been put to sleep by the necklace.

"They are fine," Levi answered. I looked at him and he was sitting up on the chair as if it was his throne. No one would ever know he was just sleeping. "Once we arrived, I destroyed the necklace and they woke up."

"And Mrs. Dennis?" I asked.

"I wanted to kill her on the spot, but she asked for forgiveness, and Abbie let her go. Though she's not welcomed here anymore."

I nodded and remembered the library. "Oh, shit, they broke the dome!"

"Abbie already fixed it."

I guess sometimes it was useful to be a witch.

I felt a little pinch on my shoulder. I glanced at it, and only saw some redness that would probably go away soon.

"I'm assuming Lacey healed me ... and changed my clothes."

"If you recall, sweetheart, I've seen you naked before, but you're right. Lacey healed you and Abbie helped her get you cleaned up and changed."

I propped some pillows between the headboard and me and leaned back. "Thank you ... for dropping whatever you were doing and coming to me."

His jaw ticked. I knew that meant he was angry or holding back, but it was so damn sexy. "It was stupid of me to go."

"Why did you?"

He stared at me. "I had business to take care of."

"Right. Big, evil demon stuff."

"Something like that."

I sighed, almost used to this. One moment, he was taking care of me, or helping me, or doing something that at first glance benefited me, and the next, he was killing innocents and torturing his enemies.

I had to remember he only came to me because of the bond.

"What did you feel?" I asked, curious about how the bond had changed. "Did it hurt a lot?" I frowned. "Wait. How did you find me?"

As usual, he looked at me and didn't answer right away, as if weighing whether to tell me the truth.

"When your feelings are intense, if I focus, I can track them," he explained. "The closer I got to you, the more I felt your emotions and your pain. It hurt, but it was tolerable."

"I'm sorry."

His brows curled down. "For?"

"For messing up the ritual, for not having broken the bond, for hurting you, for forcing you to come to me because you have no other choice." He had said the other day how confusing the bond was, and he didn't know what was real anymore.

If there was no bond, he would never feel anything for me.

All of it was the bond.

"I can handle it." His voice was tight.

"Just … hang in there, okay? I promise I'll break the bond as soon as I can, but first … I really need my magic back." My chest expanded as the feelings from last night flooded my system. "I'm so sick and tired of being a victim and needing help. I used to be so badass, and now I'm always the damsel in distress. I hate it."

"Last night, you weren't a damsel in distress."

"Yes, I was. I was able to save myself, but if I had had my magic, I would probably have not been taken. Those lion shifters would never have gotten the best of me like that."

And to think they could have done worse if they wished. They could have hurt the Evermores and Lacey, stolen precious books and dangerous items.

Thinking small, they had only come for me.

"You're doing well, sweetheart, and with the Evermores' help, you'll get your magic back soon." He was being kind and I wasn't sure I liked that. It confused me. He cleared his throat. "We can break the bond later. I'm not worried."

Why wasn't he worried? He was probably dying to get rid of me.

Suddenly, he shot to his feet and walked to the window. He opened the rest of the curtain, letting light stream in, and stood there, bathing in the glow.

It was such a beautiful scene, it was almost painful to watch.

To occupy my thoughts before he felt them, I reached for the nightstand where my cell phone was. I picked it up and cursed under my breath. The screen was broken.

"Where was it?" I asked. In the panic, I didn't even remember dropping it.

"By the bookshelves, near the stained-glass window."

Right. When I was about to hide between the shelves, and then opted for flying instead.

I gasped, remembering my wings. I reached back, to feel the faint scars on my skin. "One of my wings was broken."

Levi glanced at me. "Lacey healed your wings too."

"Can she do that?"

"She found out last night that she can."

"That's good." I almost smiled. My wings were fine, I was fine, the Evermores were fine, and even the glass dome was fine.

I threw the covers from my legs and scooted to the edge of the bed.

Levi turned fully to me. "What are you doing?"

"I'm getting up."

"But you almost died last night, and it took a lot to heal you, and—"

"Levi, I'm fine. If I stay in this bed, I'll go crazy. If you're so worried about feeling my pain, then I promise to take it slow and stay seated on a couch while I help Abbie scan through the books."

His frown was back.

I stood up, and his eyes went to my legs instantly. Oh, yeah, he had seen me in this shirt before, and he knew it was short. For some reason, I liked when he looked at me like that. It made me feel strong. Sexy.

I walked past him, my steps deliberate, and went into the bathroom.

I heard Levi's groan three seconds before the door opened and closed.

A small smile adorned my lips. Yes, the bond affected him, making him want me, but I still liked it.

Forty minutes later, I had taken a shower, washed my hair, changed into clean clothes—my usual leggings and a long-sleeved tee—and stopped by the dining room for breakfast, even though it was already late morning.

I halted two steps in and tensed, remembering the scene from last night. Light, it had been horrible, seeing all of them like that. For a moment, I thought they were dead, and it would have been because of me.

With that in mind, I ate my breakfast, which appeared in front of me, and even though it was delicious, it didn't sit right with me.

I ate quickly and went to the library, knowing I would find everyone there. Abbie was hunched over the books, Maggie was sorting them, while Lacey and Levi gathered the books on dragons. On the landing on the second floor, Belinda taught a lesson to Gwen, Britt, and Trent.

I had no idea where Magnus was and I didn't care.

When they saw me approaching, everyone stopped what they were doing.

"Ariella!" Maggie hurried to me and gave me a big hug. "Are you all right?" She pulled back quickly. "Damn, I didn't hurt you, did I?"

With a small smile, I shook my head. "No. Thanks to Lacey, I don't feel anything." I looked at Lacey. "Thank you."

She pressed a hand to her chest. "My pleasure."

I cleared my throat. "I need to say something. I'm the one to blame for last evening, and I'm so sorry. Everyone here was in danger because of me, and I will understand if you prefer I leave. I just ask you to let me continue the research somehow—"

"That's nonsense!" Maggie exclaimed.

"You're not going anywhere," Abbie said.

"But they tricked you, me, they could have—"

"But they didn't." Abbie sounded so much older than she was. "For the time being, we aren't allowing visitors."

"Again, because of me."

"Well, it has been proven to us again and again that it might not be safe to allow visitors," Abbie said. "We'll need to rethink that, but for now, we have work to do." She pointed to a chair across from the desk. "Now sit down and help me or it'll take us two years to recover your magic."

Hiding a smile, I walked to the chair, sat down, and grabbed a book from the pile.

Another thought came into my mind. "Wait, doesn't the Grand Eternity Hall have security or wards? How did those two lion shifters manage to disarm you with a necklace?" If this place was so special as everyone said, that should have been impossible.

"It turns out the wards and spells around the hall have to be replenished every couple of years, or they become less effective," Abbie said. "I learned about that last night when I picked up one of my mother's diaries." Her lips pressed tight.

"I'm glad she took note of everything in her diaries, because she didn't have time to teach me everything herself."

I almost crossed the table and gave her a hug, but she looked like she was trying to hold on, so I followed her lead. "And you spent the night redoing those?"

She nodded. "I need some special ingredients for some, and a few potions I started brewing, but later this week, we'll be all good again."

I scoffed. "They were lucky, then."

Maggie leaned closer and whispered to me, "Lucky, or they knew about it."

"Maggie!" Abbie snapped. "None of us knew about this. How could someone have told them? And no one here would have done that."

"I know, I know, but it's strange," she muttered before returning her attention to the books in front of her.

"Anyway, it's solved now," Abbie continued. "We're all safe and sound." She turned the page of her book. "And we should get back to work."

Silence reigned in the library, except for the occasional voices coming from upstairs, when one of the kids answered about their lessons.

First, I tried getting a good bearing of what was right in front of me. Abbie had separated the books about magic absorption and transference to one side of the table, the dragon books to the other, and she had lots of open notebooks and handwritten notes in between.

I read a few of her notes.

Some dark witches can absorb magic. Most of the time, it's partial and doesn't last.

Some kinds of witches can lend magic to other supernaturals for a brief period of time.

Some higher demons can absorb a supernatural's power and have it for as long as they live. But Paimon was Prince of the Underworld, he probably could do that and more.

Dragons are the most powerful supernaturals. They can absorb and return magic at will. Some dragon shifters can do something similar but on a much smaller scale.

Some fated mates can transfer magic to each other, or they can combine their magics to be stronger.

Pixies and sprites can absorb nature's magic.

It was impossible for another supernatural to hold too much dragon's magic. See about Ariella's friend.

I frowned, thinking about Raika. I had told them Raika had absorbed the entire dragon's magic and more. But I had left shortly after that, feeling sorry for myself for having lost my magic.

I didn't know what had happened after.

Curiosity took hold and wouldn't let go. I picked up my phone, walked to the far end of the long table, and sat in a chair beside the stained-glass window.

Though I had changed numbers, I had transferred most of my contacts. I confess, there was a minute there that I almost didn't, but now I was glad I had.

I called Raika's number, but to be honest, I expected her number had been disconnected, or that Shane would answer.

I was pleasantly surprised when she answered on the second ring. "Hello?"

"By the light, Raika, you're alive!"

There was silence for a moment. "Ariella? Is that you?"

"Yes, it's me."

"By the moon! We're so damn worried about you! What the hell is going on? Wait …" Her voice sounded far then. "I need to take this. I'll be right back." Five seconds passed and she continued, "All right, I'm here."

"Listen, if I caught you at a bad time, I can call later."

"No, it's fine," she said. "It's just a boring council meeting. Shane can handle it without me." I nodded to myself. "Are you okay?"

"I'm … okay. Still without my magic, but I got my wings back."

"You did? That's great!" She really sounded happy for me. "I'm glad you're calling, but I know it isn't just to tell me that. What's going on?"

"First, whatever the angels are saying, I didn't do it."

"They aren't saying much," she told me. "They haven't said anything, actually. They sent messages to the supernaturals that you're dangerous and need to be captured."

"Has the reward increased?"

"It has."

"Damn it. I'll tell you the abridged version: they are saying I killed some angels during a mission, and I didn't. I know who did and he's trying to silence me before I can tell the others why."

She was silent for a handful of seconds. "I believe you."

Just three simple words, but it filled my chest with relief. Maybe all of my friends believed me and would side with me if needed.

I swallowed the emotion and continued, "I want to expose the truth, but I can't do it without my magic."

"The magic my father took from you."

"And then you took it all from him. Raika ... may I ask how you survived?"

"Oh, sure. The dragon my father killed? She laid eggs! The goblins from the mountain found them and brought them to us. I was able to transfer the dragon's magic to the eggs."

"Oh, so my magic went to the little dragons."

"Yes, I'm afraid I was only able to keep my darkfire and wolf shifter abilities. I'm so sorry, Ariella."

"No, it's fine. If it means you survived, I'm glad they have it." It was the truth, but it still hurt.

"Is there anything we can do for you to help with your magic, with the angels, whatever?"

I considered. Too many people were involved. The less people involved, the better. At least for now.

"I think I got what I need at the moment, but thanks for the offer. If I need help, I'll call you."

"Please do. I mean it, Ariella. We're here for you."

She meant it. They all did and that warmed my heart a little more. "Thanks," I muttered.

I ended the call before she asked more questions.

My mood soured.

I glanced at the table, where all the books were, waiting for me to go back to them. I had hoped Raika would have a solution for me, but I should have known better.

Levi was beside the books, looking at me.

He probably felt disappointment in me, and the sudden will to give up on all of this. Thankfully, he didn't say anything. He picked up a heavy book and extended it to me.

With a sigh, I pushed up and walked to him. I took the book and sat down across the table from Abbie. Levi pulled up a chair, sat down, picked up another book, and started skimming through it.

I watched him for a moment. What the hell was he doing? He shouldn't be this nice to me, damn it. It made the bond act up, and my feelings stir.

His eyes met mine, the blue suddenly dark. His jaw tight, he reached for the book on my lap, opened it, and pointed to the page.

I chuckled, and I almost kept staring at him to contradict him. But I wasn't ready to deal with that can of worms, so I glanced down at the book, determined to focus.

The book was about dragon eggs and baby dragons. I frowned and considered throwing the book across the room. Instead, I took a long breath. It wasn't the fault of the little dragons that they had gotten my magic. It wasn't even Raika's. She had done what she had to survive. I would have done the same in her place.

Reluctantly, I skimmed the page.

I got to a chapter about growing eggs and slowed down to read it. Apparently, the eggs needed the constant influx of their mother's magic to grow strong and make it to the end of the cycle and hatch. If the mother died, the eggs rarely made it.

Other dragons could give them magic, but since it wasn't the same, there was still a good chance the eggs would perish.

And if other supernaturals tried to infuse them with magic, it was considered a foreign power, and the eggs stored it away, keeping the dragons safe. When the dragons hatched, this foreign magic was stored in their bones, where it couldn't hurt them.

"When a dragon dies, isn't his magic stored in his bones?"

I asked out loud. I already knew the answer, but I needed to hear it from someone else.

"Yes," Abbie and Levi said together.

My magic was a foreign power the eggs had gotten from Raika, and supposedly, it was now either stored inside the eggs, or if the eggs had hatched, inside the dragons' bones.

A feeling started deep in my gut, and I tried keeping a lid on it before I got excited and lost it.

"What is it?" Levi asked, probably feeling it.

I told them what Raika had told me and explained to them what I had just read. By the time I was done, Maggie and Lacey stood around us, listening too.

"The dragons might still have my magic," I finally said.

"That sounds possible," Abbie agreed.

"That is great!" Maggie exclaimed.

"What are you going to do now?" Lacey asked.

I picked up my phone again. "I'm going to make another call."

11

I ACTUALLY MADE TWO CALLS—ONE TO KAZ, THE DRAGON shifter I had met when we were searching for the dragon several months ago, and to Evelyn, the dark witch whose affinity was to tap into dragon's magic, especially magic stored in their bones.

Before we found out dragons and dragon shifters weren't extinct, Evelyn tracked the bones and collected them for safe keeping, as they were too powerful. She had freaked out when she met Kaz and the dragon, but I had no idea if she was still in contact with them.

Either way, I believed I needed both of them for my idea to work.

However, neither of them answered my calls. I texted, asking them to call me as soon as they could.

Because I was so impatient, I also texted Hazel and Raika, asking them if they had heard from Evelyn and Kaz, and if they could help me contact them.

Both said they hadn't spoken to them in months but would call.

Hopefully, by the end of the day, I would hear from them, and we could plan the next step.

I tried quieting my excitement and read the dragon books to make sure I understood this right—if it wasn't just outdated information—but I couldn't sit down. I needed to burn some energy.

After asking the sisters about where I could exercise, I went to my bedroom, changed into yoga capri pants, a cropped top, and sneakers, and headed to the gym room. Thankfully, it was a straight shot from my bedroom and I only took one wrong turn. I opened the door, and it was like I had stepped into another building completely.

The gym was rectangular room with smooth, black floors, three light gray walls and one mirrored wall, fluorescent lights in modern silver lamps running across the double height ceiling, a rubbery mat floor on one side and lots of equipment on the other, including treadmills, transporters, bicycles, a handful of weightlifting machines, and a shelf full of free weights. Around the perimeter of the room was a track for running.

This was amazing.

Why hadn't anyone told me about this place sooner? I would have come here every day to keep myself in shape. It wasn't easy to beat up dudes three or four times my size without my supernatural powers!

After a quick stretch, I started jogging on the track. Five minutes in and my muscles started protesting and that was why I shouldn't take long breaks. I pushed through the pain, knowing it would get better the more I ran.

I didn't know what to expect in the future. I would, hopefully, get my magic back, but that meant another fight, and I would need all the stamina I could muster.

I ran for twenty minutes, then went for the weights. I could have run more, but I wanted to restart slow and steady. If I was spent today, tomorrow would be worse.

I had done a set of exercises for my arms and shoulders, when someone entered the room.

Weight in hand, I stared at Levi. "What are you doing here?"

He opened his arms, as if showing me his ensemble. I could see the black sweatpants and the white tank that molded to his ripped chest and showed his toned arms. "I thought you could use a sparring partner."

By the light …

I put the weight down. "I'm not sure that's a good idea."

That naughty half grin of his adorned his lips and he crossed his arms, making his biceps bulge. "Why, sweetheart? Are you afraid I'll kick your ass?"

"I know you *can* kick my ass," I said.

He lifted his hands, palms to me. "I promise to behave."

I scoffed. "Do you even know how to behave?"

"I guess we'll find out."

I shook my head. "Don't do this."

"Do what, sweetheart?" He took several steps toward me. "Stand here, look handsome, and offer to help you train?"

Exactly.

"Please, leave."

"Sweetheart, I'm—"

"Levi, you're not helping."

"Yes, I am. I'm here to train." He walked to the mat, stood

in the center, brought his hands up, feet apart, and knees slightly bent in combat stance. "Fight me."

I shook my head.

A darkfire bolt appeared in Levi's hands. It flew toward me and sparked on the floor beside my feet.

"What the hell?" I cried, appalled.

Another bolt zoomed to me, and I had to jump to the left to avoid it. Then a third one at my feet again.

"Stop it! No magic!"

"Then fight me, sweetheart."

A fourth bolt flew toward my head. I had to duck to escape it.

"You ..." I groaned and rushed him.

He smiled right before dodging the punch I had prepared for that damn grin.

I did a series of quick jabs and crosses, all aimed at Levi's pretty face, but he was damn fast and dodged them all as if he was playing, which I knew he was. It only made me madder at him.

I threw a jab with my right hand. He swiftly moved to the left, but I was ready for him and kneed him in the lower back with my left knee. His eyes became two huge blue balls for half a second, then he stopped the defensive moves and changed to the offensive.

Levi punched my shoulder, hard enough to make me twist my body. Taking advantage of my position, he walked into me, making me lose balance. I toppled, but he wrapped an arm around my waist and knelt down beside me, softening my fall. I lay on the mat, Levi hovering above me, one hand on each side of my head, and his feet outside mine, in a plank that showed off his biceps, triceps, and whatever other muscles a pair of arms could possess.

"What are you doing?" I asked, my voice faint.

His eyes on mine, Levi lowered his body over me. "Having some fun."

I gulped as he pressed against me, spreading my legs beside his hips. His stomach touched mine, but he kept his chest and shoulders propped up with his arms.

My body heated instantly, yearning for him.

"Levi," I whispered, half lost to the need.

He leaned into me, his mouth dragging along my jaw. "Tell me you want this," he whispered in my ear.

I opened my mouth but couldn't speak. He pushed his hips against mine, and I felt his hard-on in the apex of my thighs.

"Tell me."

"I want it." I whimpered. "I want you."

So, so bad.

"That's good, sweetheart, because I fucking want you too." He groaned and brought his lips to mine.

Lost to the desire, I opened my mouth and welcomed him. His kiss wasn't gentle, wasn't soft. Levi was a rough man, and he took what he wanted.

And right now, I was more than willing to give it to him.

I wrapped my arms and legs around him and matched the frantic rhythm of his mouth. He moved, creating delicious friction between our hips.

With deft fingers, he pushed the straps of my top down, and his mouth followed, leaving a fiery trail on my skin.

"Y-you know this is only the bond, right?"

He licked the upper curve of my breast. "Does it matter?"

I wanted to say it did, but honestly, right now, it didn't. All I wanted was for him to feed the beast he poked and put out the damn fire threatening to explode within me. He pulled my top fully down and flicked his tongue on my nipple. I gasped and arched my back.

"Does it matter, sweetheart?"

"By the light, no!" I snapped. "Just …" I groaned. "Just take me."

"My fucking pleasure." He closed his mouth around my nipple, twisted his body to the side a little, and slid his hand inside my pants.

I squirmed and gasped in shock and pleasure when his finger found my center. Levi didn't give me time to think, to process, he simply slipped two fingers inside me and started pumping while sucking and licking my breasts.

I arched my back, giving him access to all of me. Because, dear light, it was good and I wanted to be lost in his arms. Right now, I would agree to anything as long as he kept going.

Knowing exactly what he was doing to me, Levi thrust his fingers deep, curling them at the end of the movement, pressing on places I never knew existed. At the same time, he sucked or flicked his tongue on my nipple.

I cried when he twisted his hand slightly and pressed his thumb on my clit, before rubbing fast circles around it. Somehow, the sensation flared, the blood inside my veins went from hot to boiling, and I drowned in pleasure.

Another thrust, another rub, another lick, and I exploded in pure bliss.

By the light …

While I was lost on cloud nine, Levi did quick work of taking my pants fully off, and then his shirt and his pants.

Before I could fully recover, his body covered mine again, and he slipped inside me.

I cried, the desire and pleasure starting anew. I knotted my legs around his hips, my heels digging into his hard, round ass, and my arms around his wide shoulders, and I clung to him, loving how he moved into me—fast, desperate, as if he couldn't control himself.

I liked it.

I liked it way too much.

And right now, I wanted it, this, us.

He rolled his hips, going even deeper, and I bit his shoulder as pleasure slithered up my spine.

It was too much and not enough.

"This is fucking good, sweetheart," he whispered in my ear. I turned my face to him and he captured my mouth, his kiss as rough as the rest of him.

As rough and as delicious.

Levi snaked one hand under me, grabbed my ass, and tilted it up a little. I gasped when he went deeper this way. He groaned against my mouth, bit down on my lower lip, then closed his lips around mine again.

His thrusts became even faster and deeper, and I felt myself reaching new heights.

By the light, how was this possible?

I lost control and came. Three seconds later, Levi's chest rumbled with a growl and he came too. He buried his face on my neck and held tight to me as his body shook and he slowly came down from the high.

For five minutes, we stayed like that. Him holding me, me wrapped around him, both of us spent and blissful.

But then I remembered.

The bond.

All of this was because of the bond.

I tensed and Levi pushed up on his elbows.

Without looking at him, I disentangled myself from him and rolled to my side, my back to him.

"What is it, sweetheart?"

I sat up, wishing I had a robe or a towel to cover myself. He had seen my naked body more than once, touched and licked every inch of me, but for some reason, I felt vulnerable right now.

Why wasn't I able to control myself with him? I was a grown up, a supernatural, a badass ... or at least I thought I was, and yet, I couldn't resist him.

I knew it was the bond, but I was freaking stubborn and I wanted to resist it!

"Nothing," I said, reaching for my top.

"I can feel you, sweetheart. Talk to me."

I glanced over my shoulder. Levi had sat up too and was a foot behind me, still fully and gloriously naked.

"I thought you didn't do small talk," I teased him.

"I guess our relationship is complicated, and we're a little past that now."

Our relationship ...

There was no relationship here.

"I should be able to control myself," I confessed. "But because of the bond, I can't."

He scooted closer to me. "Look at me, sweetheart." I glanced at him over my shoulder again, letting my hair fall around me and cover my breasts. "Tell me the truth ... would it be so bad if we had fun with the bond before we break it?"

I frowned. "Maybe?"

"We don't need to pretend to be a happy couple, hold hands, snuggle, or anything like that, but we can have sex like we just had." He leaned forward and pressed a kiss to my shoulder. I shivered. "Or was it so bad you don't want to repeat it?"

I rolled my eyes. He knew it hadn't been bad at all. In fact, it was hard not to jump him right now and go for round two.

"You know that's not it."

"What is it, then? Your moral compass? An angelic rule?" That wasn't it, either. Angels were more composed than most supernaturals, but it wasn't rare for angels to date around before claiming a pair. "Or are you promised to an angel?"

I smiled at that. "Angels don't do that kind of stuff."

"Then the only thing holding you back is yourself."

That and my poor heart. I knew a one-night stand or two or three wouldn't kill me, but on the inside, I was softer than I liked, and I could easily fall for him, bond or no bond.

And with the bond? It would be hard to know the difference, if there was any.

"Levi," I started.

"Sweetheart, I never had to ask or beg someone to be with me and I won't start now." He raised both hands. "I won't be upset if you say no." He said it casually, but there was a disappointed glint in his blue eyes.

I frowned. "What about the dagger? Aren't you trying to seduce me so I lower my guard and tell you where the Scarlet Hex Blade is?"

He pressed a hand to his chest. "I'm not, sweetheart. I won't press you about the dagger."

As a demon, he probably could lie right to my face and not feel one ounce of remorse.

But damn, those eyes, that intense stare.

By the light, how could I resist him?

Choosing to believe his lie, I twisted around, pressed my hands on his shoulders and pushed him down, until his back was on the mat and I was straddling him. "Damn it. Are you sure you're above begging? I wanted you to grovel."

A growl started deep in his chest. He rolled us around and glued his body to me. "Consider this me groveling, sweetheart."

He closed his lips around mine, and before I could think, he was inside me again. I gasped against his mouth, worked on building some walls around my heart and just enjoyed the ride.

12

Levi and I were the last ones to make it to the dining room for supper, and it was entirely his fault.

Well, sort of.

After we had sex for the second time in the gym, we went to my bedroom, where we had sex a third time! The man was almost insatiable and his stamina incomparable. I bet he could keep that up for a couple more rounds, and by the Light, my traitor body wanted it, but I didn't want to give a reason for the witches to come looking for us.

We took our usual places across the table from each other, but Lacey kept staring at us, her eyes knowing. Heat spread over my cheeks and Levi winked at her.

Oh, Light, I wanted to hide under the table.

Tonight, Belinda was tired and Magnus was his usual pleasant self. But other than that, everything was the same. The sisters talked about their lessons, Trent talked about his hide-and-seek game with the animals, and then Maggie explained about our discovery that could potentially bring my magic back.

"And the best part of it all," she said, "is that if this Kaz guy agrees to it, Ariella will see dragons!"

"Let's hope Kaz agrees," Abbie said. "He can't be the only obstacle for this."

"Right," I muttered. I hadn't spent much time with Kaz, but from the get-go, he had kept to himself. I was a little worried about his answer. If there would be one at all. He might never call or text me back. What if he had changed numbers like I did? He seemed keen on going into hiding with the dragons again.

"Ariella already saw a dragon," Levi said.

I looked at him and the shine in his eyes told me he had felt my sudden spiraling feelings and he had come to my rescue.

My heart squeezed and the damn bond tugged.

By the light, I was torturing myself here.

"Really?" Trent's voice pitched high.

Despite the fact that I had lost my magic, it had been a pretty fantastic sight.

I told them about our quest and how we had to fight demons who were chasing the dragon. Trent leaned closer, almost coming over Gwen and Britt, who were between us, his mouth agape, his eyes wide in wonder.

However, I lost Trent for the chocolate brownie with salted caramel that was served for dessert.

"It seems you have a new fan," Levi said, his voice low.

"New fan? You mean my only fan."

His eyes narrowed slightly, but I tried not reading much into it.

"Let me enjoy it while it lasts." I glanced at the little boy, who devoured his dessert in huge spoonfuls. "Well, I think it's already over."

Levi offered me that lopsided grin and my heart skipped a beat. I focused on my dessert and almost moaned when I took a bite.

"Okay, I agree with him. This is much better."

I glanced around the table, suddenly feeling a lot lighter, a lot happier. Everyone looked happy and well. Trent smiled with his teeth covered in chocolate, Abbie chided him, though she couldn't contain her laughter, and the other sisters laughed too. Like me, Belinda observed the others with a smile on her lips. After two glasses of wine, even Magnus seemed to have relaxed a little, though he didn't say much.

Lacey smiled a lot, and Levi seemed less like a menacing demon and more like sweet temptation. Whatever Levi and I had, it was fun and I would enjoy it while it lasted.

Seeing everyone like this brought a certain longing to my chest. I missed my friends—Farrah, Wyatt, Kayden, Lavinia, Killian, Raika, Shane ... there were so many. And I had left them all behind.

Maybe it was time to stop being stubborn and let them know I was okay, things were looking up, and I would have my magic back.

I looked at Levi and a strange force tugged at my heart at the thought of leaving him.

His eyes met mine.

I inhaled deeply, at peace, at least for tonight.

"Are you okay, sweetheart?"

I nodded. "The only thing better than this, would be if I got my sword back too."

"Oh, you lost your Celestial Sword too?" Maggie asked. Everyone's attention turned to me again.

"Yeah, a higher demon destroyed it," I said, feeling Levi's and Lacey's eyes on me. It had been Molraz, their father.

"We have a Celestial Sword here," Britt said, sounding bored.

I sat straighter. "You do?"

Everyone nodded.

"Yeah, it's on display in the Light Gallery," Gwen said.

"Do you want to see it?" Trent asked, his mouth still dirty from the brownie.

"Of course!"

The sisters and Trent led Levi, Lacey, and me to the Light Gallery, while Magnus took Belinda back to her chambers.

Once we arrived in the gallery, I understood the name. The ceiling was glass, not stained, letting pure light come in, and all the items in this gallery were about pure and light magic.

The sword was on a pedestal at the end of the large room, and I froze upon seeing it. It was a little rusty, but still so beautiful with its long silver blade and white hilt and silver details.

"The sword is old and dull, and I believe it's magicless," Abbie said.

It didn't make sense. Celestial Swords were tied to the guardians. They were made from our power, and once we died, they crumbled into ashes.

Unless they were destroyed by higher demons, something that only happened a handful of times in our long history.

"How do you have it?" I asked, my fingers itching to reach out and touch it.

"It belonged to an angel, friend of the family, several hundred years ago," Maggie said. "He asked our ancestors to enchant it right before he died, so the sword would live on forever."

"From what we read, he hated the idea of the sword disappearing," Gwen said. "He didn't like that it would be sitting here, but wanted it to survive his death."

"Can't you take it?" Trent asked, amused.

My eyes widened for a moment. "I probably can't. I mean, it was another angel's. It's tied to his essence and I'm sure it wouldn't work."

Abbie's brows curled down. "Maybe we can make it work."

My breath hitched. "What?"

"I can't guarantee anything, if it'll even be possible," she continued. "But maybe we can enchant it. Make it answer your call. It won't be exactly like a Celestial Sword, but it can be yours."

"This sounds like a challenge," Britt said, sounding interested.

"I like this idea," Lacey said. "Can I help?"

"Of course," Gwen answered. "But first, we need to clean it.

The sisters laughed.

Abbie looked at me. "It's your call."

My chest tightened. "Are you sure?"

"Of course." She jerked her chin to the sword. "Take it."

With trembling hands, I stepped closer and reached for the sword. It was heavier than mine had been, a little longer too, it was a little dirty and rusty, but by the light, it was a freaking Celestial Sword and it could be mine.

"How does it feel, sweetheart?" Levi asked. His eyes were brilliant as if he was enjoying this. Perhaps he was because he couldn't help but feel what I felt.

I held on tight to it. "Amazing."

"Come on." Abbie beckoned us to the door. "Let's get started."

13

I STIRRED IN BED AND TURNED, ALMOST LANDING ON TOP OF Levi.

After the witches gave me the Celestial Sword, we took it to the lab—a huge greenhouse with long wooden tables, vials, and tools. The witches prepared potions, studied plants, and came up with new herb-related spells there.

I put the sword on a corner of the table Abbie had cleared for it, and the witches started by analyzing the sword, sensing its dormant magic, making a list of what needed to be done.

They decided to leave the sword bathed in moonlight water to clean it of any impurity, visible or not.

"This will take all night, perhaps all morning too," Abbie warned me.

And somehow, shortly after that, Levi and I ended up in my bedroom.

Now, it was early morning, and I couldn't help but look at the sleeping man beside me. His face was turned to the side, facing me, his arms crossed as if he was arguing with me, his head rested on the pillow, and his face was calm, serene, and yet still menacing.

I believed he looked malicious all the time because his features were cut so sharp, so hard, so damn sexy.

I inched my hand closer, wanting to trace his full lips, his straight nose, his thick eyebrows, his chiseled jaw. His damn body. With his arms crossed, his thick biceps and wide shoulders were tight, the muscles contracted, and his chest was puffed ... and the rest was covered by the thin comforter.

But I had seen it all, touched it all, and by the light, how could he satisfy me like nothing else, and it still not be enough? I could probably have sex with him three hundred times in the next month, and I would still want more of him.

My body heated up at the thought. Levi stirred, his brows curling, probably feeling what I was feeling through his dream.

To let him rest, I slipped out of the bed, reached for a silk robe in the closet, grabbed my phone, and went to the bathroom. I brushed my teeth, washed my face, and stared into the mirror.

Five years ago, I thought I had lost everything when Molraz destroyed my sword, ripped my wings, and killed my friends. It got worse when I found out the angels thought I was the one behind that failed mission and the murderer.

Then it got even worse when I lost my magic six months ago.

But finally, finally things were looking up.

I had my wings, I would have a new sword in a matter of hours, and hopefully in a couple of days, I would have my magic back.

After that, hell would probably break loose until I found

out what was going on and how to fix it, but for now, I would be glad for my wins.

I ran a hand through my long silver-blond hair. It used to have curls, but in the last five years, my hair had straightened out, as if protesting not being an angel anymore.

That would all change soon. Would my hair change back?

I almost laughed. Who cared? My hair wasn't that important.

I reached for my phone to look at the time and saw a text message.

I opened it and almost squealed—it was from Kaz. He had sent it late last night, and somehow it had gotten through. Maybe he had sent it as I was walking by the library to come to my bedroom. I typed a text back, but of course, there was no service here.

Shit.

Trying to be as quiet as I could, I slipped into the closet, got dressed in a new pair of tight jeans and a black sweater, grabbed my boots, and sneaked out of the bedroom.

It was just past six in the morning, so I was the only one in the library. I put my boots down, ignored them for now, sat down, and called Kaz.

The phone rang four times and I was about to put it down when he finally answered.

"Hi, Ariella."

A wave of relief washed through me, but soon my stomach tightened. Yes, he had answered, but it didn't mean he would agree to my plan.

"Kaz ... I need your help."

I explained to him about what happened to me—he had been there, he knew—and how Raika was able to survive after giving the dragon's magic to the eggs. Then I launched into what I had read about the foreign magic being stored away from the dragons.

"Is it true? Do you know? Could my magic be somewhere inside the eggs, tucked away to be discarded?"

He let out a sigh. "It's true. If Raika gave the eggs all of the magic that didn't belong to her, then that means the dragons now have your magic and everyone else's Paimon stole."

I shot up and started pacing around. "Do you think there's a way for me to get it back?"

He paused, probably considering. "There might be."

I almost cried happy tears but inhaled deeply to calm myself. "Explain might."

"Of the eight eggs, one didn't make it, three hatched, and the other four are still eggs," he said. "We will need powerful witches versed in dragon magic to be able to coax your magic out of the dragons and the eggs *without* harming them."

"I sent a message to Evelyn," I said. "She hasn't replied yet."

"Evelyn is an expert in dragon magic, but not strong enough."

I frowned. "What if I get you a strong witch and Evelyn. Do you think that would work?"

He didn't answer for six full seconds. "I need to talk to the council. The other dragon shifters and dragons are even less keen on mixing with other supernaturals than I am. I can't promise I'll convince them."

Shit. "But you'll try?"

"I will talk to them. But again, I can't promise anything."

I nodded. "That's enough." For now, at least. "And I'll call Evelyn."

"If I get approval from the council, I'll try contacting her too."

"Kaz, thanks."

"Don't thank me yet."

But I thanked him again before we ended the call.

I felt like running, dancing, shouting, singing, even though I believed Kaz and knew it would be tough to convince the dragon shifter council.

But even if they said no, we could keep bothering them, presenting better solutions, until they agreed. If I had to, I would wait until all the dragons hatched.

Hopefully, though, that wouldn't happen and I would have my magic back soon.

I paced, incapable of containing myself. No one was here, our research was mostly done, and I didn't know what to do. I could go for a run, train a little.

Or ...

I went back to my bedroom, walking fast, trying not to run. I burst through the doors, and Levi was exiting the bathroom.

"Morning, sweetheart," he said, with a lazy grin. "I was wondering where you were."

I stopped long enough to admire his fine, naked body. But only for about ten seconds. "Morning," I said as I took off my sweater and went to him.

One of his eyebrows shot up, but he wrapped his arms around my waist when I was in arms' reach and pulled me tight against him. "Insatiable, sweetheart?"

For him? "Always."

I rose on my tiptoes, but Levi met me halfway. Holding me, he carried me backward to the bed, where he made quick work of getting rid of my clothes and extinguishing the fire the way only he could.

———

I LAY HALF BESIDE AND HALF OVER LEVI, MY ARM FOLDED ON HIS chest, my chin on the top of my hands.

He propped some pillows behind his back and looked at me. "Are you going to tell me what has you in such a good mood, sweetheart?"

I smiled, still feeling exhilarated about my phone call with Kaz and about what we had done in this bed. I told him about the call, while Levi ran his fingertips up and down my back. I didn't think he noticed what he was doing.

What he was doing to me.

Yes, the lust, the want ... it was the bond.

But was it *all* the bond?

I wasn't sure anymore and I guess I never would be.

"That's good, right? He'll call and you'll get your magic back."

My smile widened. "I can't wait."

His intense eyes met mine, and suddenly, they darkened.

"Sweetheart," he started and I tensed. "There's something I should tell you."

I pulled away. "Hm, nope. We're not doing this."

His brows curled down. "What do you mean?"

"This ..." I pointed to me and him a couple of times. "It's casual. It's fun. Let's not bring personal stuff and secrets into the mix."

"I'm involved in a lot of your personal stuff."

"Well, I was the one to come to you for my wings and my

magic, so that's on me. But it's fine. We've established we're enjoying the bond while it lasts, right?"

I put on a brave smile, but inside I was cracking and I knew he could feel it. I wanted to be a strong, badass angel, but I had feelings too, and it was really hard to put them aside most of the time. But I tried. I forced them to the back. Because if I didn't, then I would certainly get hurt again.

"Right," he said, his jaw popping again. He sat up on the bed. "I'll just say this once: I think you'll want to know about this."

"Is it about my magic? About my sword? About my wings? Does it involve Rhodes and his betrayal?" Or assumed betrayal. I still didn't have all the facts. "Or the dragons?"

"No."

I shrugged and got up from the bed. "Then I don't want to know."

I started building the wall around my heart faster. Soon, the bond would be broken and he would leave. If this wall was only half built by then, I would crumble.

I knew I would.

"Just remember you're the one who didn't want to know," he said, his voice low as he stood from the bed and walked into the closet.

I reached for my clothes on the floor and started putting them back on. Why did I feel like a bitch right now? Wasn't I doing him a favor? He was the one with the cold heart who didn't want to get involved. He was the one who had said we could keep this casual.

In ten seconds, he would come out of the closet with that charming grin of his, call me sweetheart, and carry on as if nothing had happened.

I was zipping up my boots when I remembered something. "Levi? When I called you when the lion shifters were attacking me, you said it wasn't a suitable time to talk. You were in the middle of something."

He came out of the closet, wearing navy slacks and a white button-up shirt. I stared for a few seconds, wondering how the hell he managed to look like he was always coming out of a magazine cover photoshoot.

"Yes," he said, not charming as I thought he would be by now.

"Don't you have to go back to whatever that was? I mean, it sounded important, but you left it behind."

For me.

"My demons took care of it."

"Ah." I nodded. "That makes sense."

We finished getting ready in tense silence, and I almost took back what I said. Almost. Obviously, I didn't want him to leave, but I didn't want to be the thing that held him back either.

Determined to be strong, I walked out the door and turned to wait for him.

Levi walked out but pointed the other way. "I'm going to stop by my bedroom. I'll meet you in the library later."

"Oh. Sure."

He nodded once, then whirled on his heels and walked away. I looked at his retreating back until he turned a corner and disappeared from sight.

I had tried to protect my heart, and this was probably him protecting his. The bond affected him, though I was sure he had much better control over it than I did.

It was okay.

Actually, this was how it was supposed to be. We had been spending too much time together, sleeping in the same bed, touching after having sex. That only strengthened the bond.

And hurt us more.

I inhaled deeply, wishing I could breathe in courage and strength, and marched to the dining room for breakfast.

14

BREAKFAST WAS DELICIOUS, BUT FOR SOME REASON, IT STILL SAT heavy on my stomach. Maggie, Trent, and Belinda were there with me, and they were as chipper as always, chattering about how the sword would soon be ready, and they couldn't wait to see it.

I couldn't wait either.

After breakfast, Belinda took Trent to do some chores, but the little boy promised to come soon to see the sword, and Maggie and I headed to the library.

There, Abbie stood beside the long tables, passing along lessons to Gwen and Britt. Lacey was reading a book about dragon eggs.

I glanced around, but I already knew Levi wasn't here.

A pang cut through my chest.

No, I wouldn't feel sad or disappointed. He said he would meet me here later, which meant it could be in an hour or five. He was nothing to me. Just a hot body to have fun with.

That was the tenth time I told myself that this morning.

What was it that people said? The more I repeat it, the greater the chances I would believe it.

I let out a sigh.

"Off with you two." Abbie shooed Gwen and Britt away, then smiled at me. "I think your sword is ready. Want to see it?"

"Of course."

"I want to see it," Gwen said.

"Me too!" Britt whined.

"All right, but just for a minute." Abbie lifted one finger. "Wait here."

She walked between two bookshelves.

I glanced at her sisters. "Where is she going?" The way to the greenhouse wasn't through the shelves.

"She's the hall's favorite," Britt said with a little disdain.

"Well, she's the heir," Gwen mumbled.

"That means, the hall gives her shortcuts and magical doors," Maggie explained. "And only Abbie."

The Grand Eternity Hall and its living magic never ceased to amaze me.

A minute later, Abbie returned holding something large wrapped in a black cloth. She deposited it on a cleared part of the long table and pulled the corners of the cloth away.

My breath caught.

The Celestial Sword shone against the dark cloth, its silver blade and white hilt clear of any rust and dirt.

"It's so pretty," I whispered.

"The sword is infused with magic, but there's one more thing we need to do." Abbie beckoned to me. I lay my hand on top of hers. She pinched my fingertip and I hissed when it felt like a prick. She pressed my finger on the blade, smearing it with my blood. The blade shone and the blood disappeared. "There. Now it's attuned to you."

I frowned. "How does it work?"

"With the magic we put in it, the blade is supposed to feel lighter than it actually is, and it's stronger too," Abbie explained. "It will take a lot to break or destroy it."

"It also should cut through almost anything," Maggie added.

"Right." Abbie nodded. "And it will answer your call. Just summon it like you would your first Celestial Blade."

It was too good to be true.

I stared at the sword and wished for it to disappear.

It trembled, as if not used to it, but after another try, it blinked into oblivion.

The sisters and Lacey cheered.

With a smile of my own, I extended my hand and called it. The sword blinked into existence, the hilt in my grip and the shiny blade stretched in front of me.

"This is amazing," I said, my throat closing with emotion. "Thank you."

"Our pleasure," Abbie said, and the sisters nodded.

I stepped away and swung it a few times, feeling its weight, its movement. It felt lighter and quicker than it should and it was awesome.

I smiled wide, so dang happy. "Thank you," I repeated.

Abbie waved me off. "It was fun for us, you know. We love a challenge." The sisters nodded in agreement. She then turned to Gwen and Britt. "All right, done here. You two, go study."

Gwen and Britt stomped away, complaining about not being part of all the cool stuff.

Abbie sighed. "And I wish I had more time." Maggie stared at her, and the two of them shared a look that probably ran deeper than we realized.

As the oldest, they both carried a lot of responsibility for the hall and their siblings.

We heard a ding. Abbie, Maggie, and Lacey checked their phones. I put my gorgeous sword away before reaching for mine.

"It was mine," Lacey said. She looked at me. "It's Levi. He said he had something to do and will be back soon."

Oh.

My chest constricted.

Why did this hurt so much?

I shook my head. Nope, I wouldn't feel anything. I couldn't. I had been the one to push him away, and I was glad he had accepted it.

We were getting too close, too attached.

It was better this way.

It was better this way.

It was better this way.

How many times would I have to repeat those words to convince myself?

Abbie reached for a book on the table. "Ariella, should we continue researching about the dragons, maybe find another solution if the dragon shifter doesn't reach you?"

"Oh right!" A little bit of excitement made its way through my chest as I told them about my phone call with Kaz. "Kaz said that if the council will allow me to go to the dragons, we'll still need a powerful witch to help us out." I looked at Abbie. I knew Lacey was powerful too, but Abbie being the hall's protector had to be more. "Will you go with me?"

She smiled at me, a true, big smile I hadn't seen from her yet. "Of course. Meeting dragons would be a great honor."

"Not fair." Maggie pouted. "I want to go too."

"When Kaz calls back, I can ask him," I said. "It isn't up to me but I'll see what I can do."

Maggie beamed. "Yay!"

I looked at Lacey and she seemed a little sad. "Do you want to come too?" Her eyes lit up and she nodded. "I'll ask about you too. Well, at least I can argue that we'll have plenty of powerful witches to help out." I pointed to the books spread over the table. "He did mention it would be good if the witches involved knew about dragons."

Lacey and Maggie reached for books, sat in chairs, and began reading.

I laughed.

And I stopped when my phone rang.

I reached for it, almost dropped it, and answered without looking at the screen, sure it was Kaz.

"Ariella?"

I frowned, recognizing the voice. "Erin? Everything okay?"

"Yeah, probably," she said. "Sorry, I got your number from Hazel, but I really need to speak with you."

15

IN THE END, ERIN ASKED TO MEET TO TALK. "IT'S IMPORTANT," she insisted.

I had to ask the sisters where their portals could take me, so I could agree on a location with Erin, but Abbie said they could open a portal and bring Erin here instead.

"Are you sure?" I mouthed.

She nodded.

I explained to Erin about the portal. Abbie said she just needed a picture of the place. Erin snapped a picture of Rey's office at the Blackthorn Hunters Academy, and then Abbie effortlessly opened a portal.

Erin and Rey stepped into the library and the first five minutes was of them gawking at the place, in awe. In the next five minutes, I explained to them what I was doing there and what was going to happen next.

"It sounds promising," Rey said. He was a half demon, son of one of the Princes of the Underworld, and current headmaster of the Blackthorn Hunters Academy. He was tall with dark brown hair and gray eyes.

"It sure does," Erin said. "I'm glad it's working out."

Erin was one of the best demon hunters out there, and the daughter of the previous king of the underworld. She could have ruled the underworld, but she had passed the baton to her half brother, Tanner, and half sister, Jasmin. She formed a beautiful pair with Rey, with her long black hair and golden eyes. I had heard both of them shared what was called a Soul Bond, a type of bond certain demon hunters shared with one another, and it was like a fated mate bond.

I gestured to the chairs around one of the less crowded tables. "Please, sit."

Rey and Erin sat down side by side, and I took the chair across from them. Abbie, Maggie, and Lacey remained at the other table, reading their books.

"All right, I'm getting straight to the point," Erin said. "The angels came to see us."

I almost fell off my chair. "What? Who? Why?"

"It was three archangels," Rey said. "Rhodes, Sariel, and Arien. They wanted to talk about our roles in fighting evil in the world."

I frowned. "Against evil supernaturals?"

"I think they meant all evil, even humans," Erin said.

I inhaled deeply. "And?"

"That was the extent of the conversation," Erin said. "They formally invited us to a summit. All of their best guardians will attend and they wanted us to bring our best hunters."

"According to Archangel Rhodes, angels have stepped back to allow demon hunters to do most of their work and they believe we've done a poor job of it," Rey said, annoyed about that. "Now that there are more demons roaming the Earth, they want to be more active."

"Basically, they want to discuss our roles and decide how to proceed in the future," Erin said.

I shook my head. "This doesn't feel right."

Erin nodded. "I know, that's why I wanted to talk to you."

"Do you know these archangels?" Rey asked.

"Yes," I said. "Rhodes is the one who betrayed us. He's the one who was leading the mission when he joined forces with a higher demon and killed all of my friends." I gulped. "I was the only survivor, and since then, he has been after me to silence me."

"That's what the reward is about," Erin said, her voice low, shocked.

I nodded. "I have no idea what's going on in Elysium right now. I don't think any outsider knows, but it can't be good. Inviting you to a summit to discuss your roles feels like a trap."

Rey's hands clenched into fists. "You think he'll attack us."

"I think that he'd set a trap to lure you in," I said.

Erin flinched. "That sounds extreme for an angel."

"How do you think I felt going on my first mission, just to see him side with the demon and kill his own kind?" My voice was harsher than I intended, but I couldn't help it.

"I hear you." Rey looked at Erin. "We should consider this."

"We can push back the summit several weeks," Erin said.

"And if they insist, we'll go prepared," Rey suggested.

"That's better, but I would advise you not to agree to the summit at all," I said. "Or agree but don't go. Observe from a distance, if you can, to see their reaction. That should tell you their true intentions."

"That makes sense," Rey said.

"I'm about to get my magic back," I told them. "When I do, I plan on going back to Elysium to find out what's happening. Push the summit back or cancel it until I can see what's going on with my own eyes."

Erin sighed. "I can't believe we're talking about angels here. Aren't you supposed to be kind, strong, and righteous?"

I scoffed. "I would love it if that was true, but no, not guardians, at least not most of us. We all have a streak *of unwanted* feelings inside us, and we're taught how to channel those feelings and use them to our advantage."

"Fuck," Rey muttered. "Since we took over the underworld, demons and evil are everywhere, and demon hunters are having a tough time fighting them all. When the angels came to us, I was relieved. I thought we could create a great alliance with them and fight together."

"I'm sorry," I said. "Maybe once I find out what's going on, we can come up with a plan together."

Erin looked at Rey, then back at me. "I'm glad we came before agreeing to the summit."

"Me too," I said. Then an idea sparked in my mind. "You don't have any other contacts with the angels, do you?"

Rey and Erin shook their heads.

"From what I know, angels stepped back a long time ago, and let demon hunters deal with almost everything on Earth," Rey said. "There hasn't been any contact since."

Erin nodded. "This is the first time in decades, maybe centuries, that the angels reached out to demon hunters. Why?"

"Just wondering if there was some way for us to find out what's going on up there sooner." And less risky than sneaking into Elysium.

"Sorry," Erin said.

"That's okay. We'll figure it out. Just don't be alone with the angels," I said, realizing my words sounded ridiculous. Angels were supposed to be the most trusted and honorable supernaturals out there. "If you must, be prepared and bring backup."

They assured me they would, and after we concluded our talk, they kept gawking at the library. Maggie asked if they wanted a short tour of the hall; Erin and Rey accepted.

Lacey tagged along as Maggie led them out of the library, and I approached Abbie, who was still reading.

"You heard, right?" I asked.

Abbie lifted her gaze to me. "The angels setting a trap for the demon hunters? That's worrying. But I think you are right. That's exactly what they are doing and the demon hunters need to delay this as much as they can."

A bout of frustration hit me hard. "I hate that I'm in the dark here. If only I could contact someone in Elysium ..."

"Who?" Abbie asked. "You can't trust anyone there right now."

That couldn't be true. There were plenty of good angels up there, angels who would repel Rhodes and his plans, if they knew. Unless they had all been captured or killed by him already.

I pressed a hand to my chest, thinking about my mother and my sister.

Nothing would change between now and later, but at

least later, I would have my magic back and could defend myself if things went sideways.

I hoped.

I felt restless and worried.

If Levi was here, I would have invited him to take me to my bedroom to take my mind off things, but since he wasn't …

And that hurt. What the hell? He had left without saying goodbye. Without warning me. I shook my head, pushing those thoughts away. No, I wouldn't go down that path.

He didn't owe me anything, much less an explanation for his actions.

If he wanted to leave and never talk to me again, then so be it.

Wound up, I decided to go to the gym and run. That was the only way for me to burn off this pent-up energy.

I started to tell Abbie where I was going when my phone beeped.

I looked at it and gasped.

It was a text from Kaz:

The council agreed. Let's meet.

16

THE NEXT MORNING, ABBIE OPENED A PORTAL TO SAVANNAH, Georgia. She crossed it first, then Lacey and I came last. Maggie stood there, watching us with a pout. She had wanted to come, but Kaz had only allowed two of them, and Lacey pulled the longer straw.

We crossed the portal onto a private pier—Kaz had sent a picture of the pier to us—at sunset. We glanced around, but there was only sand and ocean nearby.

And a demon.

Levi stood on the pier, waiting for us.

I frowned at him, surprised and a little irritated. "What are you doing here?"

He flashed me that incorrigible half grin. "Protecting your pretty ass, sweetheart."

As I suspected, whatever had happened yesterday was forgotten and he was back to his annoyingly charming self.

"I told him where to meet us," Lacey explained. "He's strong. If anything happens, we'll need his help."

I frowned. Nothing would happen, other than meeting

the dragons and getting my magic back. Unless we did something to offend the dragons, and Kaz had no other choice but to attack us.

Which was ridiculous and wouldn't happen.

I stared at Levi, trying to control my feelings. Right now, I was mad at him, and yet I couldn't help noticing how good he looked. He wore a black suit, a dark teal shirt with two undone buttons, and no tie. His hair was combed back, showing more of his handsome, dangerous face.

"I know it's entertaining to stare at me, sweetheart, but don't we have a meeting to get to?" he asked, still smiling.

By the light, I wanted to punch him.

Suppressing a groan, I let my wings out. Levi took off his suit jacket and his shirt, handed them to his sister, and called on his wings. They were bigger than mine, and bat-like, with talons on the joints and tips.

I pushed off, flapped my wings, and took to the sky. Levi followed me, a few feet behind. We flew low, near the water, in case there were any boats on the ocean.

We followed Kaz's directions, and sure enough, about ten miles off the coast, we saw a small island. It was round with sparse sand, a rocky shoreline, and little vegetation. If I had to guess, I would say the entire island was about ten acres in area.

In the center of the island were five stone pillars in a circle, and right beside them was Kaz and two other dragon shifters, Evelyn and Ash.

Levi and I landed ten feet from them.

Evelyn smiled at me. "I see you got your wings back."

I tucked them behind my back. "I did."

She stepped forward and hugged me tightly. "It's good to see you."

Ash came to us and patted my shoulder. "Everyone is worried about you."

I almost rolled my eyes. "I know, but I'm good, I promise."

I pulled back to see Kaz fuming at me. "I think I said only you and two witches."

Kaz was an impressive dragon shifter. Tall and wide, wearing a leather vest that showed off his toned arms, and a large crossbow on his back. He had long brown hair on top with the sides shaved short, his eyes were dark green, and he had a light red scar across his left eye and eyebrow.

"I know but—"

"I'm Leviathan, a higher demon, and I'm bonded with Ariella," Levi said, in his most charming voice. "I'm here merely for her protection."

"Is this true?" one of the other dragon shifters asked.

"Yes, we're bonded," I said, the words sour in my mouth.

Evelyn looked at me as if she wanted to know how that had happened. I wasn't sure I wanted to tell her.

"Ariella, this is Trolin and Velak," Kaz said, gesturing to the two older dragon shifters. Trolin had auburn hair tied in thick braids, and Velak had the sides of his head shaved and the remaining black hair in a mohawk. "They are part of the council."

I frowned, taking in their leather clothes, their weapons, their hair. These dragon shifters sure looked like Vikings. I made a mental note to one day, when things were peaceful again, look up if there were any historical connections between Vikings and dragon shifters.

"We're here to make sure you don't take more than you

need," Trolin said. Clearly, Kaz had to convince them to do this.

"I assure you I won't," I said, firm and yet gentle.

I closed my hand around the coin Abbie had given me and the portal opened. Abbie and Lacey stepped through, and I introduced them to everyone.

"Wait." Ash frowned. "The Grand Eternity Hall is a real place?"

Abbie nodded with a proud smile.

"What is the Grand Eternity Hall?" Evelyn asked.

"It's a place of great knowledge and power," Abbie said. "Imagine the ultimate supernatural library, museum, and prison all into one."

"Wow." Evelyn glanced at Ash. "And you knew about this place?"

Ash nodded. "Yes, my mother and sisters mentioned it a couple of times. Apparently, some old and powerful grimoires are in here, and they often joked about trying to steal them."

"We do have many powerful grimoires," Abbie said. "And thankfully, none have been stolen."

"Oh, I would love to see those someday."

Trolin and Velak cleared their throats.

"All right, we should get started," Kaz said. "Evelyn and Abbie will perform the spell. Are you all ready?"

"Give us five minutes to talk about it," Abbie said, approaching Evelyn.

The two of them walked among the five pillars, followed by Lacey and Ash, and I took a good look at the place. The pillars were made of smooth black stone, like the floor among them.

"Is this a special place?" I asked Kaz.

"It's a meeting place," he said. "For when we need to talk to other supernaturals."

Right. Because the dragon shifters and the dragons didn't want anyone to find their mysterious hidden island. For good reason. I bet dragons would be in terrible danger again if everyone knew where to find them.

Speaking of which ... "Where are the eggs and the little dragons?"

Kaz took a large step to the side, allowing me to see past him. Down a short hill were the four eggs and the three little dragons playing with each other.

One was a dark blue, the other was a dark green, and the third one was black. Their scales were shiny, and they looked like oversized stuffed bears—but with sharp teeth and a breath of fire.

The blue one jumped on the green one. The green let out a small puff of fire that touched the tail of the black one, who turned to the other two and lunged, biting the wing of the blue one. They rolled together, play-fighting like any other animal.

It was a magical, surreal moment.

"They are incredible," I whispered.

"They are." Kaz crossed his arms. "You should have seen Evelyn when she first saw them. She freaked out. Even Ash did."

"Has she visited your island?" I asked, my gaze on the little dragons.

Kaz shook his head. "No, the council won't allow it."

"She's a witch, a stranger," Trolin said, his tone harsh. "We don't allow outsiders in."

"But she calls when she finds bones with magic, so I can take them to the island and give them a proper rest," Kaz said. "We always meet here."

I nodded. Poor Evelyn. It must kill her to know there was a hidden island out of reach where the creatures she loved so much lived together.

"Here," I heard Abbie say.

I glanced at them. The three witches finished drawing a pentagram on the smooth black floor connecting all five pillars. Evelyn put small white crystals on the inside corners of the stars, Lacey spread some powder along the lines, and Abbie placed a pink crystal the size of a football right in the middle of the pentagram.

"We're almost done here," Evelyn announced.

At that, Kaz and the other dragon shifters went down the hill. They picked up the eggs, while talking to the little dragons. The black one snapped at Kaz, but Kaz was firm with him, and he dropped his head low.

Reluctantly, the little dragons followed the men to the pentagram. Kaz and the others put the eggs down, right in the center, and Kaz told the little dragons to step in and stay.

My nerves picked up as the witches grabbed my shoulders and pushed me inside the pentagram too, right beside the dragons and the crystal. I stilled as they looked at me, their heads tilting to one side or the other, curious. The "little" dragons couldn't be more than a few weeks old and they already reached my chest. If they stretched their necks up, I bet they would be taller than me.

"This should be simple," Evelyn said. Right. Because everything in my life had been simple so far. "I'll pull the magic out of the dragons, and as it's coming out, Abbie and

Lacey will split it. Ariella's magic will go back to her, and the rest will go to the pink crystal."

Since we were taking my magic out, Kaz had asked if we would take all of the foreign magic from the dragons and the eggs. But I also didn't want any magic that didn't belong to me, especially because Paimon probably had absorbed a lot of dark magic, and I didn't want to deal with that.

So, Abbie had brought a special crystal where they would store the foreign magic, and then she would take that to the Grand Eternity Hall and hide it from the world.

The witches stepped out and stood outside the drawn line while the others—Levi, Ash, Kaz, Trolin, and Velak stayed outside of the circle created by the pillars.

I glanced at Levi, knowing he could feel how nervous I was right now. His brows were curled tight, but his gaze never wandered away from me.

"Ready?" Abbie asked.

I inhaled deeply and nodded.

The dragons looked at Kaz. "Just stay there," he said, then repeated it in their language.

Evelyn, Abbie, and Lacey held hands, closed their eyes, and Evelyn started speaking Latin in whispers—the spell.

A hum started under the pentagram and the magic swirled around us. The eggs trembled and the dragons squawked.

"I can feel it," Evelyn said, her eyes still closed. "There's a lot of foreign magic here." Her brows turned down. "I got it from the eggs!"

The pink crystal shook and then I felt something, like an invisible snake, slithering around my ankles, up my legs, around my middle. I did my best to stay still, but my nerves were frayed and I didn't like the way this magic tightened around me. It wrapped around my chest and my shoulders, covering every inch of me. Then, it pressed against me. I groaned as the magic seeped through my skin and my muscles, pooling at my core.

I wobbled with the sudden burst of energy inside of me.

"No! Stay back!"

I looked at the voice and saw Lacey pointing her finger at Levi, who was halfway from the pillars to the pentagram, his eyes on me.

"I'm fine," I said, my voice rough. Honestly, I wasn't sure what I was feeling yet. Was I fine? I seemed to be.

"We're not done yet," Evelyn said. She kept her eyes closed and I knew she was going for the dragons. She groaned and the dragons squirmed beside me.

"What are you doing?" Trolin asked, his voice high.

"I'm not hurting them, I promise," Evelyn said. "It's just … I can feel the magic, but it's hidden." She groaned more and the little dragons let out faint cries. One flapped his wings, almost knocking me out of the pentagram.

"Hang on," Kaz told them. "Just a little longer."

"There!" Evelyn said. "Found it." In my mind, I imagined Evelyn's magic wrapped around the foreign magic like a hand grabbing a piece of fruit, and then pulling it out of the bag.

The dragons squawked again, jumped, flapped their wings. The dark blue one let out a small cloud of smoke from his nostrils, and the dark green one sent a thin jet of fire toward Evelyn. Lacey put it out before it reached them.

"Almost there," Evelyn said with a groan.

The black one let out a cry and jumped at me. I took a small step back, careful not to leave the circle and raised my hands. He closed his mouth on my lower arm and twisted.

I cried and fell to my knees, and the dragon let go of me.

A darkfire bolt zoomed where the dragon's head had been. I snapped my head at Levi, who was standing a few steps behind the witches and ready to send another bolt if the dragon tried anything.

"Don't," I told him, my gaze firm.

By then, Kaz had reached him, and the two of them started arguing about it.

I tuned them out, then finally, the dragons stopped and the invisible snake once more wrapped around my legs, torso, arms ... this time, it was stronger, tighter, and I felt like I was sinking into the depths of a dark ocean.

The magic pushed inside me, found the other pieces, and when they came together, my chest seized in an implosion and I fell back at the pain. My vision went black and my breath hitched.

"Ariella!"

I didn't know who had screamed, but suddenly, everyone hovered over me.

Levi was the closest. Knelt beside me, he pressed a hand to my forehead. "Can you hear me? Sweetheart?"

I tried nodding, but that only made my head hurt.

"What's going on?" Lacey asked.

"I think," Evelyn started, "that after months divided, her magic had some sort of burst when they joined again."

Abbie nodded. "That's possible." She held the pink crystal and it pulsed with supercharged magic. She put it inside a bag and slung it over her shoulder. She patted it, as if making sure it was still there.

I inhaled deeply and felt my magic stirring inside of me, a little lost, a little rebellious, and a little afraid. But it was my damn magic, I knew it, I could feel it, and it made me happy.

I held on to Levi's arms. He understood what I wanted and helped me sit up. I looked at my hands and saw a faint glow to them. My chest squeezed with relief, but then soreness spread through me. The glow disappeared.

That was when I saw the bite mark on my lower arm and the blood staining my sweater. It stung, but it wasn't as bad as I thought it had been.

"Lacey," Levi said.

"On it." She knelt on my other side, gently got my arm in her hands, and healed the bite. The sting was gone, but the soreness continued.

"Can it hurt her?" Levi asked.

Evelyn shook her head. "No, it shouldn't. It is her magic."

"But it can feel strange for a little while," Abbie said. "It's like when you don't exercise for several months, and then suddenly you're back, and everything hurts and you're weaker than before."

"Yeah," Evelyn said. She knelt beside Levi and looked at me. "Your magic will probably feel unstable for a while. I suggest you train so you can get used to it again."

"And the magic to you," Abbie added.

Evelyn nodded.

Levi's eyes roamed over my face, my body. "Are you okay, sweetheart?"

I took another deep breath. This time, nothing really hurt, I just felt the soreness, but if I had understood what they were saying, that would stay until I started training again.

"I'm fine," I said, my voice rough. "Help me up."

In one swift movement, Levi supported my back and pulled me up. He kept one hand on my lower back as I glanced at everyone around me. "Thank you. Seriously, this means a lot to me." I made a point to look directly at Kaz and Evelyn and hold their gazes for a few seconds. "Thank you."

Evelyn smiled. "My pleasure."

Kaz nodded. "This was in our interest too. I could feel the foreign magic in them. It bothered them, but I couldn't take it out. It also never occurred to me that some of it was your magic."

"I'm glad we helped each other, then," I said.

"Are we done here?" Trolin asked, sounding bored.

Kaz looked at Evelyn and me.

"I think so," I said.

"We are." Kaz turned to the other two dragon shifters and the three of them picked up the eggs and ushered the little dragons. "We're going home now."

Kaz and the other dragon shifters released their leathery wings.

A sound like a rocket cutting through the air echoed through the island, and we all looked up as a dozen angels flew toward us at impressive speed.

Kaz turned to me, his eyes pained. "I have to keep them safe."

"Go," I told him. "Be safe."

They pushed off and flew away, in the opposite direction from the angels. Though two of them broke off from the group and went after the dragons.

"No," I whispered. I started calling my wings, but Levi was faster.

"I've got this," he said as his wings appeared behind his back. He zoomed after them.

I felt divided, wanting to help, but the angels landed not fifteen feet from the rest of us. I recognized Julien, Izrail, and Mihael, who had been hunting me a few weeks ago. And right in the middle was Archangel Sariel. My father had been her mentor after she graduated from the academy. When my father died, Rhodes became her mentor.

"It has been a while, Ariella," Sariel said with a friendly smile.

"Not long enough," I said. "How did you find me?"

"We've been looking all over for you," she said. "There are plenty of supernaturals helping."

"Someone saw me," I said.

She shook her head. "Actually, this time, I sensed your aura a few hours ago."

My eyes widened and I felt so stupid. Lacey had told me I wouldn't need to drink the potion to hide my aura while I was in the Grand Eternity Hall. I had gotten used to it, and on my first foray outside, I forgot to take it!

"Lucky you," was all I said, though I was berating myself on the inside.

"I don't have time to waste, so I'll get directly to the point," she said. "Come with us and we won't hurt your friends."

Which meant, if I didn't, they would kill everyone.

Beside me, the witches conjured bolts of their magic and held them above their hands, and Ash drew his sword.

"I guess you have your answer," I said, reaching for my magic, but it swirled out of reach. Damn it!

"So be it!" Sariel snarled and lunged at me, light magic shooting out of her hands.

At the same time, the other angels attacked and my friends met them head on.

I jumped back, avoiding a big bolt that would definitely have hurt, and called on my new, beautiful sword. I almost sighed in relief when it appeared in my hand.

Sariel, though, seemed taken back and she slowed down her momentum. "I heard you lost your sword." She brought hers up and then down on me.

I parried her strike. "You mean, Rhodes told you Molraz destroyed mine?"

"Something like that." She stretched her arm, her hand glowing, and tried touching me.

I pushed her sword with mine and kicked her hand away. "So, you're Rhodes's lackey now?"

That seemed to anger her. She let out a scream and threw her magic at me. I spun to the side and deflected one of the hits with my sword. I braced myself, expecting to be pushed back, but the blade absorbed most of the impact.

I almost laughed. Light, this sword was awesome!

Sariel let out a furious groan and threw several light bolts at me, one after the other. I moved my sword, trying to catch them all, but she was too fast.

I twisted out of the way, but she followed.

I called my magic and created a shield. Or tried to.

The magic sparked at my fingertips and then fizzled out.

What the hell?

Sariel came at me, her sword raised high. She rammed into me, making me lose my balance and fall on the rough ground. I kicked her shin, and she stumbled back.

I looked to the sides—Levi wasn't back yet, and everyone

was engaged in a fight. Two angels were on the ground, immobile, and my heart sank.

No one should die, especially not an angel.

This was so wrong.

Sariel brought her sword up again and let out a scream as she brought it down on me. I moved as fast as I could, came up to my knees, and lifted my sword above my head.

The sword clanked and shook with the impact.

I stood and kicked Sariel in the chest.

She staggered backward, and almost lost the grip on her sword.

"I don't care if they want you alive," she said with a cry. "I'm done with you." She conjured a light bolt and threw it at me.

I lifted my sword.

A big shadow fell over me; Levi stood between Sariel and me in his demon form. He deflected Sariel's magic with a blade made of darkfire.

She stared at him, her eyes wide.

"Levi!" someone shouted.

I followed as Levi glanced to the voice—Abbie. She nodded at him once, and he nodded back.

What?

Before I could ask anything, Levi sent out a wave of dark-fire, tall and powerful. It hit the angels and flattened them to the ground. Darkness was left in the wave's wake, thick and potent. He had used this once to hide us from supernaturals at a park.

He grabbed my hand and pulled me with him.

A few steps to the side, all of our friends gathered in a circle.

Abbie opened a portal. "Hurry, let's go."

17

WE RAN THROUGH THE PORTAL AND INTO THE HALL'S LIBRARY.

I turned to the portal, ready to impale whoever else came through, but it poofed from existence.

Levi, Lacey, Abbie, Evelyn, Ash, and I looked at each other, all of us huffing as if we had run a marathon.

Then Lacey pressed a hand to her stomach and she dropped to the ground. Levi was fast and softened her fall before she hit her head on the floor.

We all rushed to her. My sword disappeared from my hand and I knelt beside Levi. I pulled Lacey's hand back, her fingers stained with blood. A big gash cut through her middle.

"Lacey?" I called out, my voice trembling. "You have to heal yourself."

"She can't," Levi said. "She can only heal others."

That was ...

"Let's take her to the infirmary," Abbie said.

Lacey groaned as Levi picked her up, but she was out of it. We all followed her through the dizzying corridors until we entered what looked like a waiting room with couches and armchairs. Abbie gestured for Levi to walk past an archway, which opened to a large room with a dozen or so beds, all with curtains separating them.

Levi deposited Lacey on a bed in the far back, closest to a shelf-lined wall full of herbs and potions.

Abbie pulled the curtain around the bed. I wanted to follow them, but she looked at us ruefully and said, "You should take care of yourselves."

Then she disappeared behind the curtain.

I frowned. What did she mean? Then I looked down at myself and saw a few scratches on my arms and hands. Evelyn and Ash, who had come with us, were also hurt.

Evelyn pointed to a counter beside the archway. "I see some supplies there."

We walked to the counter and cleaned up our wounds in silence, but listening to the grunts and groans from Lacey, while Abbie did what she could to help her.

Could Abbie heal Lacey? I knew her gift was herbs and potions, and I truly hoped that was enough.

I closed my eyes and focused on the bond. It was faint for me, fainter than I thought it was for Levi, but when I reached for it, I could feel his despair, his pain, his fear.

He was scared for his sister, and he hated that he could do nothing for her.

A hand clutched my chest. I wanted to go there and hug him, hold his hand, tell him it would all be okay.

Because it would, right?

It had to.

I turned to the back of the room, intent on being with him, when Maggie rushed through the archway. She pointed her finger at us without even looking and said, "Stay there," and disappeared behind the curtain with the others.

I stared at the plain curtain for a moment. Had the sisters communicated telepathically? Could they do that? Otherwise, how did Maggie know we were here?

A few seconds later, Gwen and Britt were there too, but the two of them didn't join the others.

"Do you need any help?" Gwen asked, taking the healing paste from me.

"Hm, unless I have a wound on my back, I think I'm good," I said.

Still, Gwen applied more of the paste to my cuts and bruises, while Britt handed something for Evelyn and Ash to drink. "It's to help with healing," Britt said. "And pain."

Evelyn sniffed it. Right. When I first met her, Evelyn ran an apothecary. "Valerian root, turmeric. What else is in here?"

"Our magic," Britt said. She handed me my potion.

"And you are?" Ash asked, taking the vial from Evelyn.

"Oh, you don't know," I said, realizing Evelyn and Ash hadn't been here before and didn't know the sisters. "This is Gwen and Britt, and the other girl is Maggie. They are Abbie's sisters, and heirs to the Grand Eternity Hall."

Evelyn's eyes widened. "Oh, that's where we are?"

I nodded as I drank the potion. Instantly, I felt the potion tingling and spreading over my body, soothing.

A sudden, loud cry came from the back of the room, and we were all startled.

"It would be better if we went to the sitting room," Gwen said, ushering us out. "Or maybe the library."

"That's a place I would like to see," Ash said.

We followed Gwen and Britt to the library. On the way,

Ash drank a big swallow from the healing potion, then offered it to Evelyn, who took one too.

The library was empty, no sign of Trent and Belinda, or even the animals.

Gwen and Britt pointed out the tree, the newly redone dome, the stained-glass window, and the different collections hidden among the endless shelves.

I stopped at the table where the books about magic absorption and dragons still lay. I reached deep within me and felt my magic stirring in my chest, slowly filling my veins.

I lifted my hand and light magic enveloped it.

Despite everything, I smiled.

"Oh my, you got your magic back!" Gwen said, her eyes wide. She smiled and walked back to me. "That's amazing!"

Britt nodded. "Impressive."

I almost rolled my eyes at the teenager. She was probably a handful to her older sisters.

I let that feeling sink in for a second and my chest contracted with pride, relief, and joy. "I'll be honest, I hoped this day would come, but it was a tiny, tiny sliver of hope."

Evelyn hugged me. "I'm happy for you."

Ash put a hand on my shoulder. "Congratulations."

"Thanks." I looked at her and Ash. "Thanks for helping me with this."

"You helped so many of our friends," Evelyn said with a small smile. "It was time someone helped you." Her shoulders sagged. "I'm sad that we needed to flee so fast. It's the first time Kaz has let me see the dragons, and I wanted to spend time with them."

"We can bother Kaz until he lets you see the dragons again," Ash said.

"I'm sorry about that," I said. Everything had been going so well, I had forgotten to take the potion, and as soon as I was out in the open, the angels found me. "It was my fault the angels cut our time short."

"At least they arrived after the spell was done," Ash said.

Evelyn nodded. "True. If they had interrupted it, I doubt the little dragons would have let us try again."

"I was going to wait until we hear from Abbie, but I can't take it," Britt said. "Tell us what happened."

"Please," Gwen added.

So, we did.

We told them everything from the moment we got to the island, to when they came to us at the infirmary.

"Do you know how she's doing?" I asked the witches.

"She's going to be okay," Maggie's voice startled me. I turned and saw her entering the library and walking toward us. "Abbie was able to channel Lacey's healing magic. She's weak, and still hurting, but she'll be fine. We gave her a sedative to truly rest, so she'll be out for a while."

"That's good news." I let out a long breath, then realized she was alone. "Where's Levi and Abbie?"

"Abbie is still hovering over Lacey," Maggie said. "And Levi was with her." I bit the inside of my cheek. "Go. I think he needs you."

I nodded and turned to Evelyn and Ash. "Will I see you later?"

"Maybe?" Evelyn said, glancing at Ash.

"They will be here." Maggie took over, sounding like a mini-Abbie, which was so unlike her. "Why don't I give you a quick tour of the Grand Eternity Hall, and then we'll stop by the dining room. I bet everyone is starving."

Gwen leaned closer to them and whispered, "The dining room is the best room in this entire place."

I chuckled. "It probably is."

With that, Maggie guided them farther into the library and I dashed to the infirmary. I had just come from there, but I was sure I would get lost again in the hundreds of endless hallways, especially because I wasn't thinking right. Because if I had been thinking, I wouldn't go to Levi, not with this desperation, this need to see him. I tried telling myself this was the bond and I should resist it, but how could I? I still could feel his fear, and now it had mixed up with exhaustion.

I entered the infirmary, expecting to find him with Lacey, but he was sitting on one of the couches in the waiting room, his elbows on his knees, and his head in his hands.

My heart tugged.

He looked up, his blue eyes dull. "Hey." I didn't think. I went to him, pushed his chest back, and crawled onto his lap him, straddling him on the couch, and wrapping my arms around his shoulders. He let out a soft scoff. "Careful, sweetheart, or I'll think you care."

"Just blame the bond," I said, trying to play it lightly, but I felt him tensing under me. I squeezed him harder, though I was sure he barely felt anything. "How are you?"

Finally, his arms wound around my waist and he buried his head in the crook of my neck. "Better now."

"What can I do for you?"

"You're already doing it," he said, his voice muffled against my skin.

We stayed like that for a little while, until I felt his fear lessen a little, but his exhaustion was increasing.

I was about to suggest he go to his bedroom to sleep when Abbie walked out of the infirmary.

Levi jumped up, holding me by my waist and setting me down beside him. "And?"

"She's fine, Levi. I told you before," Abbie said. "And she's stable. Let her rest for now."

Levi groaned.

"I'll make him behave," I said.

Abbie offered me a tired smile. Then, she patted the bag, which was still slung across her torso. "I have a powerful and unstable crystal to lock away." Right. The crystal with foreign magic. I had already forgotten about it. "I'll come back in a couple of hours to check on her."

I nodded and Abbie walked out without another glance at us.

Levi fell back on the couch and I stood there, not sure what to do next.

With a growl, he grabbed my arm and pulled me back to him. "Where do you think you're going, sweetheart?"

I adjusted my legs and arms around him. "I was here."

"Hm." He held me tighter. "I could feel you were confused, probably thinking about leaving."

"Aren't you? Confused I mean?"

He pulled back and looked at me. "Right now, all I want is to stay like this. If it's the bond, I don't care."

"Levi, about that ..."

He tensed again. "What?"

"We can talk about it later." I started pulling away from him. "I can feel you're tired. Why don't you go rest and later—"

"No." He held my arm and kept me on his lap. "Tell me now."

Shit. "It's just ... I promised to find a way to break the bond after I got my magic back."

"And that is done."

"I know your head is focused on Lacey's health now, but I can start researching. I bet the sisters will help me."

"What about your plan? To go to Elysium?"

"Yeah, I mean, that's the plan, but I've been in this mess for five years already, what is a few more days? Besides, I think it would be better for us to have this bond cut when I go."

"Why? Are you planning on dying there?"

I flinched. "Of course I'm not, but what if it happens? Or if I get hurt? I don't want you hurting too."

"I'm a big boy, sweetheart. I can take it."

I frowned. "Levi—"

"I know going to Elysium and finding out what is happening is important to you, Ariella. The bond can wait."

"But ... are you sure? I thought you wanted this gone."

He stared at me for a long time, his jaw ticking. "I do. I want it gone, but the bond has been there for about a month. You've been waiting to get your wings back for five years, your magic for one. Get this over with, then we'll worry about the bond." His jaw relaxed and his lopsided grin took over. "Besides, aren't we having fun?"

I scoffed. "You and your dirty mind."

He leaned into me, one of his hands closed around my nape, the other slipped under my pants and reached for my ass. I gasped and he whispered in my ear, "Sweetheart, you have a mind just as dirty as mine."

I turned my face to his and he captured my mouth, his kiss hard and harsh as always.

Levi broke the kiss and stood up, holding me against him. He moved both his hands to cup my ass, and I locked my ankles behind his back while he walked out of the infirmary and into the room across the corridor.

It was a large parlor restroom, with a foyer area with a chaise lounge and a golden framed standing mirror. A little farther was the counter with dual sinks and ornate golden faucets, and beyond that, a closed golden door for the toilet area.

Levi pushed me against the wall and glued his body over mine.

"I thought you were tired," I said, knowing his exhaustion had taken a backseat to the lust that had burst from the both of us.

"So tired," he joked right before pressing his mouth on mine again.

I kissed him back for ten seconds, then I placed my hands on his chest and pushed him back.

He let me and looked at me with puzzled eyes. I spun us around, pushed him against the wall, and reached for his pants. He leaned into me, trying to capture my mouth again, but I knelt in front of him.

His eyes went wide for two seconds, then a half smirk spread over his lips.

I pulled his pants down, enough to free his erection.

By the light, he was huge.

I closed my hand around the shaft and licked the tip slowly. A hiss came from Levi and he leaned against the wall, as if he needed the support to stay standing.

Hm, I had barely started and he was already like this?

I liked it.

I closed my mouth around the tip and sucked.

Levi let out a string of curses.

I smiled as I took him fully in—a feat, considering how big he was. I started moving, my mouth and hand in sync, working him up.

"So fucking good," he whispered as he knotted one of his hands in my hair and guided me to take him even deeper.

I let him, but after a few strokes, I took control again, going faster and sucking harder. Levi's body shook and he cursed again.

Then he hooked his arms around my shoulders and pulled me up. His eyes shone with raw desire. "That was amazing, sweetheart, but that's not how we're going to finish this."

With a naughty grin, he held my gaze as he took off his shirt and pants completely. He jerked his chin, and I shook my head and did the same. Then he spun us around, pressing my back against the wall again. None too gentle, he grabbed my leg, brought it up around him, and slid inside me.

He groaned, I moaned, and then he was moving.

With another groan, he closed his mouth around mine and kissed me, the rhythm of his lips matching the rhythm of his hips—fast and deep.

I had learned by now, there was no other way with him.

And I was fine with that.

So damn fine.

I held on to his wide shoulders and brought my other leg up, knotting my ankles behind his back. At this angle, he went deeper and it was so damn delicious.

"Fuck," he muttered against my mouth.

He braced a hand on the wall, the other closed around my waist, as he pumped inside me, taking as much pleasure as he was giving. I should be used to it by now, no? To how good this felt, to how hot, exciting, and delicious having sex with him was.

I felt it deep in my veins, in my core, and I had an inkling that a lot of this could be the bond. I had always heard that when you cared for someone, sex was even better. I cared for Levi. I mean, I didn't wish him anything bad, but I bet the bond increased this feeling tenfold, confusing me.

I played dumb because I didn't care.

As long as he kept having mind-blowing sex with me, I didn't care one bit.

Then suddenly, Levi let out a groan, pulled back, dropped my legs down. I was about to complain when he spun me around, so I had my hands on the wall and my back to him.

He grabbed my waist and slid inside me from behind. He hissed and I gasped. He went deep and hard and fast from the get-go, and it was so, so good. This angle, this position, it was different and somehow, even better.

I braced against the wall, arched my back, and tilted my hips up a little.

"Hell," he muttered as he went even deeper.

One of his hands snaked up and cupped my breast as he pumped into me, sending tendrils of fire and pleasure through every inch of me.

By the light, how could this be so damn good?

He leaned over me and ran his tongue over my spine, making me shiver from head to toe.

"You're delicious," he said, his voice hoarse.

He was too, and I wanted to tell him, but then he slid his other hand around my hips, down my belly, and to my core. He flicked my clit and I moaned as my legs almost buckled under me.

"Keep going," I said, breathless.

Levi obliged and even increased the pressure of his fingers on my clit—and I broke down with a cry. He wrapped an arm around my waist, leaned over me, thrust hard three more times, and let out a groan when he came.

After a few seconds, the tremors in his body slowed and he pressed me fully against the wall, his body glued to my back.

"Delicious as usual, sweetheart," he whispered in my ear.

18

WE DIDN'T SNUGGLE OR PRETEND TO BE ANYTHING MORE. After having sex, we got dressed and left the restroom. Levi had become unsettled again and insisted on checking on Lacey. And I went with him.

I hesitated when he reached for the curtain. He turned to me and frowned. "It's not your fault."

"She went there because of me."

"She was helping a friend," he said. "I bet that even if she knew what would happen, she would have chosen to go anyway."

He pulled the curtain halfway and stepped around it. I took a handful of slow steps and stood beside the bed. Lacey was sleeping, her skin pale, but otherwise, she was clean, wearing a hospital gown, and a white blanket was folded to her chest.

I touched her covered legs. "I'm sorry for this but thank you for helping me." I glanced at Levi. "You too. Thank you."

A corner of Levi's lip curled up. "Anything for you, sweetheart."

One of the strings around my heart pulled hard. I knew that was the bond talking, and what I felt toward it was also the bond, but I couldn't help being confused.

With a sigh, Levi sat down in an armchair.

"When was the last time you ate something?" I asked.

"Last night? Maybe breakfast this morning."

I frowned. "I'm starving. I'll go get something for us."

He nodded, his eyes half closed. I knew that the moment I turned my back, he would fall asleep. I was tired, but I was still on cloud nine for having my magic back, and I couldn't stop thinking about the next steps. I needed to act *now*.

I stayed there for five seconds, taking him in, imprinting his beautiful face on my mind. I was going to see him again, but it was probably when we were ready to break the bond.

I smoothed my hand over Lacey's knee and whispered, "See you later."

As silently as I could, I walked out of the infirmary and headed to the dining room and stood by the table. A second later, two plates with yummy sandwiches appeared, along with a glass of juice.

I smiled, always in awe that the hall knew what we wanted.

"Myg?" I called, knowing that the hall would warn the goblin if she was far. Thirty seconds later, Myg shuffled her big feet into the dining room. "Could you take this sandwich and drink to Levi in the infirmary, please? If he's sleeping, just leave it beside him."

"Yes, angel," the goblin said, deadpan.

"Thank you."

Myg snapped her fingers and Levi's food disappeared. She

turned and left through the back door, but I was sure she could get to the infirmary from there. Somehow.

I sat down and ate my sandwich by myself, while desperately trying to just enjoy the amazing food and keep my mind clear, which was almost impossible.

I swallowed the last bite and went to my bedroom, where I packed my stuff. I made sure to take the aura-muting potions with me, at least a handful, in case my magic was unstable.

I also borrowed a couple more leggings, shirts, and sweaters from the vast closet. I doubted they would miss these pieces, and I was in desperate need of more.

I slung my duffel bag over my shoulder and turned to the doorway, dreading going to the library and facing the witches. I opened the door and came face-to-face with Abbie.

"I was coming to find you now," I said.

"I know."

I frowned and stepped back. "What do you know?"

She walked in, her gaze fixed on my bag. "That you're leaving and that you would rather do it quietly than say goodbye to everyone."

I did hate goodbyes. "How do you know that?"

"I'm connected to the hall in more ways than you think." She halted a few steps in and faced me, her delicate brows curled down. "Your magic is unstable; I can still feel it. You're welcome to stay and train with us until you feel you have control over it."

A small smile spread over my lips. "Thank you for the offer, really, it means a lot to me, but I think I'll ask someone else to help me." I had just the angel in mind.

"I see you've made your decision."

I nodded. "I have."

"Well, if you're ready, I can open a portal for you. Where do you want to go?"

Since I hoped to ask for help from someone located at DuMoir castle, I probably should be close to them. "Hartford in Connecticut. Ever been there?"

Abbie shook her head. "No, but I've been in Boston or New York."

"I think Boston would be closer."

"I remember the Public Park very well. Will that work?"

I nodded. "It'll probably be easier to hide a portal there than in a museum or library."

"I can make portals invisible, so that's not a problem."

My eyebrows shot up. Seriously, these witches, this place … it kept on amusing me.

Without ceremony, Abbie opened a portal and gestured toward it. "Here you go. Just … take these." She deposited a handful of silver coins in my hand. "You're welcome here anytime. Just say *fores*. A portal will open and you'll arrive at the library."

"Thank you." I closed my hand around the coins. "And thanks for everything. Please thank your sisters and everyone else. What you've done for me, I won't forget it."

"You're very welcome."

I hesitated. Should I hug her? Say more stuff? I wasn't good with goodbyes. I hated them, but I couldn't leave without her help.

In the end, I nodded my head once at her and walked through the portal.

I glanced around, but only saw trees. Great. No humans had seen me. The portal disappeared and my chest tightened.

It was okay. This was part of the journey. We were moving forward.

I channeled my magic. It trembled in my veins, but I felt it right there, alive as if it had been switched on. Inhaling deeply, I dug deeper and felt as if it muted my aura. Perfect. Now, hopefully, no angels could find me.

But as far as I knew the reward was still on my head and I could walk by a bad-intentioned supernatural at any time.

So, I pulled my leather jacket's hood over my head and hid all of my hair before walking past the trees. A few yards away was George Washington's statue. All right, now I knew where I was. I found an empty bench under a tree, sat down, and fished my phone from my pocket.

Soon, I would fall from exhaustion, but until then, I didn't allow myself to stop. Why go bury myself in an inn and sleep while I could get something done?

I didn't have his phone number, but I knew someone who had it.

The phone rang once before her voice came from the other side.

"Ariella? Is that you?"

"Hi, Queen Thea, yeah, it's me."

"Holy night, we've all been worried about you," Thea said. She was the Witch Queen of the Silverblood coven, and fated mate to Drake, the Lord of DuMoir castle. Together, they were probably the most powerful supernatural couple of this century.

Stronger than them, only their daughter, Aurora—a half vampire, half witch destined to be the Queen of All Witches. The little, beautiful girl was probably eight now, maybe nine, and she already had a big destiny laid out in front of her.

"I'm fine; everything is fine," I said. "Before you ask anything, just know I'm innocent of whatever is being said about me."

"Oh, we know that, even though the angels won't say what crime you committed. Just that you're guilty and dangerous." She scoffed. "So much bullshit." Then she gasped. "Never thought I would say that about angels."

I chuckled, though there was no pleasure in it. "I know. I've been having contradicting feelings about them for years now, to be honest."

"I'm sorry. It's not easy to feel like an enemy to your own kind."

I nodded, knowing she spoke from experience. "Thea, you've probably guessed I called because I need something."

"I did. What do you need?"

"I would like Zadkiel's phone number, please."

"Of course. I can send you his contact via text, is that okay?"

"Yes, that works."

"May I ask why you want to talk to him?"

"Well, I got my magic back."

"You did? That's wonderful!"

"Yeah, but it's unstable, and I need to train it a little before I try using it."

"Oh, so you thought Zad would be a good choice, since he's also an angel."

I nodded to myself. "Exactly."

"Well, I'll send you his contact information, but he and Elisa are on a mission for the next two days. Try calling him. If he doesn't answer, leave a voice message, or send him a text.

I'll warn Drake you're looking for him, so when Zad reports, Drake can tell him. If that's okay?

My shoulders deflated. So even if I spoke to Zad, he wouldn't be available for the next two days. "Oh, yeah, that helps for sure."

"Wait, where are you staying?"

"Hm." I glanced around, but only saw more of the park. No inns or hotels or anything like that that I could see from here. "Nowhere at the moment."

"Then come to the castle. Are you near?"

"I'm in Boston."

"Oh, that's an easy two-hour drive. Get a car. Borrow it if you have to. Come here."

"But ... if I go to you, the angels will see it as you choosing a side."

"Which was chosen long ago when we befriended you. Ariella, you want to train with Zad. Where else will you do it? Just come here."

It did make sense. Instead of holing up in a hotel waiting, I could go to somewhere I knew, where I felt safe, where my friends were.

"All right," I said, feeling suddenly lighter. "I'll borrow a car."

"Great! I have a class at my school soon, but I'll make sure everyone knows you're coming. If you're arriving here in two hours, then you'll arrive before dinner. You can have dinner with us!"

"Sounds good. See you soon."

I turned off the call and let out a long breath. Then I called Zadkiel. Like Thea guessed, he didn't answer, but I left a voice message, and I sent him a text.

My plan was to hopefully train with him for a day or two, enough to get a handle on my magic again, and then I would be able to go to Elysium.

Excitement bubbled in my veins as I stood from the bench and walked toward the street. I needed to find a quiet parking lot, choose a car, and borrow it.

If Levi was here, he would rent one for me with his endless fortune—

I halted those thoughts before they went further. I wouldn't think about Levi, even if the bond was faintly tugging at my chest for me to go back and check on him.

I had a mission to focus on.

I didn't have to walk far to find a three-story parking garage. With a trick of magic light, I slipped through the main entrance without drawing attention. I hid behind a pillar, pointed my finger at the lights overhead and the only security camera there, and blasted them with magic. It was a little stronger than I wanted, and instead of flickering lights, the bulbs exploded.

It got the attention of the two guys in the main office. When they went to check on the exploding lights, I grabbed a handful of keys, and moved to the back of the garage, where there were no security cameras.

Hoping the guys couldn't hear it, I pressed the keys and listened for the beep. After about five tries, a car near me beeped—a black, compact crossover. More than enough for me.

I dropped the other keys beside a pillar and reached for the car's door.

A tingling sensation traveled up my spine and I froze.

Slowly, I turned.

Five supernaturals stood several yards from me, spread out in the open space, blocking the exit.

Shit.

I inhaled deeply and allowed my magic to do its thing. The two women were vampires, one of the men was half fae, and the other two were demons, or half demons.

"We found her," one of the women said.

"You're the angel they are looking for, right?" the half fae asked. "What's your name? Adrienne? Andressa?"

"No, Chris, it's Ariella," the other vampire said.

Chris, the half fae, nodded. "Right, that. Ariella."

"You know what we're here for," one of the demons said. "So, let's skip the part where you resist and we kick your ass, and just come with us."

A little excitement warmed up my blood as I channeled my magic. Even if it was unstable, I could use it. And if it got out of hand, I had my sword.

I let light cover my hands. "You should skip the part where you talk."

I threw bolts of light at them. I hit one of the demons, while the others spread out. The vampires were on me in two seconds, while the demons created darkfire. I summoned my sword and slashed the vampire's arm before she could reach me. The other lunged for my throat, but I lifted my hand and blinded her with my light.

I spun away from the darkfire and used the blinded vampire as a shield. Several bolts hit her chest and she trembled with the impact. The vampire with the arm cut groaned and swiped a claw at me. I swung my blade up, cutting her arm again. She rammed into me. I let go of the other vampire, who was unconscious, and turned my blade to her. When she leaned into me, I plunged it into her chest, right through her heart. I knew that was probably not enough to kill her, but that should be enough to stop her.

A darkfire bolt zipped past my head and I again used the vampire as shield. I pulled my sword back and she fell at my feet.

The demons cast bigger bolts and I created a light shield in front of me. Beside the demons, the half fae recovered. He joined forces with the demons and threw fire at my shield—a Blaze fae.

The bolts kept coming and my magic trembled in my veins. I tried holding on to it, but it fizzled out. Then it exploded and a bright light erupted through the parking garage.

I stumbled back over the car's hood, my head a little dizzy. Dang, that was strong. I blinked fast, trying to recover before my enemies did. The explosion had hit them. One of the demons was on the ground, struggling to get up.

The fae and the remaining demon renewed their attacks, sending more darkfire and fire at me. I tried creating another shield, but my magic didn't obey me. I ducked out of the way and hid behind a column. Their bolts chipped away bits of cement with every hit.

I couldn't count on my magic right now. I needed to find a way to get closer to them and stop them from using their own magic, so I could use my sword and get this over with.

I lifted my hand and called my magic. Even if I could cast a bolt of light, or blind them, that would be enough time for me to get to them.

My magic flickered around my fingertips. I yelled, stepped away from the column, and threw a bolt of light at them.

Just then big light bolts came from their side and took them down. They groaned, trying to come up, but the bolts kept coming. After a short volley, they stayed down.

What ...

Then someone rushed forward but halted when she saw me.

My eyes widened and I whispered, "Ylena."

19

I couldn't believe my eyes. "Ylena? What ...?"

"Thank the light you're okay." She rushed to me, her white-blond hair in a loose braid, and hugged me tight.

I stood there, shocked. This woman, this angel, had been my mentor for so long. I had looked up to her for most of my life, and once I was cast out, I sometimes thought that I would never see her again.

"I ... How are you here?"

She pulled back but held on to my hands. "I ran away."

I looked into her pale blue eyes. "What? Why?"

"Rhodes attacked me."

I gasped. Ylena was one of the most powerful archangels in Elysium. In all of the best scenarios that played out in my head, I went to Ylena, told her about Rhodes, and she captured him and stopped his plan, whatever it was.

"Ylena, what is going on?"

"I don't know," she said with a cry. "When he came back from your mission, five years ago, he told me you made a deal with a demon and you killed all of them. He got away because he was stronger. I didn't want to believe him but there was so much evidence. And you had run off."

"Which made me seem guilty."

She nodded. "I'm sorry. I should have known."

"All right, so, you believed him and sent angels to hunt me."

"At Rhodes's insistence, Adona ordered us to send angels to Earth to capture you. You were to be brought back for questioning."

I scoffed. "Questioning, my ass. Rhodes wants me dead."

She nodded. "I know that. He said ... by the light, he has gone crazy. In the last few months, he has been babbling about a reform, how we need to change the structure of our hierarchy, and then he asked me to join him. To take over Elysium and purge the world of all evil. Including evil angels. There are no evil angels!" She shuddered. "It was horrible."

A reform? That sounded as bad as I had imagined. "You said no and he attacked you?"

"Exactly! Many of the archangels are on his side, along with other angels." A sob escaped her throat. "He has been working on this for years, and I had no idea. How could I have been this blind?" She inhaled deeply. "I gathered a few angels who were on my side and we fled but most of them died during the escape. The remaining ones and I decided to spread out and look for you. We know that you're an important piece of this puzzle, or he wouldn't be so desperate to find you."

"He's not after me." I shook my head. "He wants something I have."

Her eyes widened. "What?"

I pressed my lips tight. It wasn't that I didn't trust her, but I didn't want to talk about it here, out in the open.

"We should go." I gestured to the car. "We can talk more when we're away from here."

"Good idea."

We moved the disabled supernaturals out of the way, hopped in the car, and exited the garage.

At first, I drove around, toward the nearest interstate, though I was going with the flow and heading out of the city.

After a few tense minutes, I glanced at Ylena. She didn't look like the powerful archangel I'd admired my entire life. She looked like a smaller, dimmer version of herself. Whatever Rhodes had done to her, he had scared her.

"We need a plan," I said. "We need to gather the angels who came with you and hash out a plan to take Rhodes and his allies down."

"Agreed."

"But first ..." I gripped the wheel tight. "You might not know this but I lost my magic about six months ago."

She gasped. "What? How?"

I told her a sixty-second version of the events. "I just got it back, but ... it's unstable. We can plan, but before we do anything, I need some help."

"You want to train."

I nodded. "Yes. I think that one or two days of training will be enough. I'm sure it's like muscle memory. I just need to exercise it."

"Are you asking me to train you, Ariella?"

"Can you?"

"It would be my pleasure." She offered me a smile. "I can contact the other angels and ask them to meet us. Where?"

I handed her my phone. "Find a motel or inn along the road, away from the city, and tell them to meet us there."

She grabbed the phone as if it was a ticking bomb. "I don't know how to operate these very well."

I almost chuckled. "You can do it."

I gave her instructions and she followed them. She found a motel thirty minutes from here, then she pressed her fingers to her temples and used one of her archangel powers: being able to send mind messages to other angels when linked before a mission.

That was smart of her. If it had been me, I would have forgotten to do that.

"One of them is only three hours from here," she said. "But the others are farther away."

"It's okay. That will give us more time to train."

"True."

I frowned, thinking. "So, after my last mission, Rhodes came back saying I was a murderer and had allied myself to a demon. And, as far as we know, he started working on the sidelines to reform our society."

She shook her head. "I would guess it takes a lot of time and patience to change someone's mind, and if he was trying to gather an army, it was probably even harder."

"But to what end? Kill Adona? Oh light, Adona probably thinks I'm a murderer."

"Adona always told us to bring you to her," Ylena said. "Like me, she thought his story was missing important pieces." She turned her torso to me. "You said before that Rhodes was after something you had, not you. What do you mean?"

Why was I hesitating? This was Ylena, for light's sake.

"The Scarlet Hex Dagger. Apparently, the entire mission was to secure the dagger from Molraz. I took the dagger and hid it."

"The Scarlet Hex Dagger? Why would he want it? Do you know what it does?"

I shook my head. "I have no idea, but if the dagger is important to his plans, it must be powerful."

"That makes sense." Ylena sighed. "And you have the dagger now?"

"It's hidden."

"Of course. Maybe we should study it and find out what it does. It could come in handy."

I frowned. I didn't like the idea, but maybe we should consider that. "First, we should focus on my training and a plan where we don't use objects we don't know." She smiled at me. "What?"

"You've grown these past few years," she said, her tone dreamy. "You've become a strong woman."

"Emphasis on woman like a human." I flinched at my words. There were times when I didn't think I would ever be anything else again.

I took a deep breath. That was in the past. I was a full angel again, a cherubin, and with Ylena by my side, I now didn't need to sneak into Elysium to find out what was happening.

With her insight, the handful of other angels who had come with her, and maybe some of my friends, we could stop Rhodes before he made a bigger mess of everything.

My heart squeezed thinking of Adona.

Thankfully, it sounded like she was safe and unaware of what was happening. I could only hope it stayed that way.

"Nonsense," Ylena said. "You're one of the strongest angels I know. I was always sure you would become an archangel someday."

A sliver of pride bloomed in my chest. "Thanks."

"We'll fix this, and everything will be right again." Ylena sounded so sure. "We'll get Rhodes and his—" She pressed her lips tight and shook her head. "I still can't believe this is happening. Rhodes is breaking my heart. I never expected this from him."

I knew what she meant. I had never been close to Rhodes, or to any higher-ranked angel, only Ylena because she was my mentor, but I certainly had thought of Rhodes as a hero, a legend.

And now he was plotting against his own kind.

As we approached the inn, a new thought struck me and I felt ashamed I hadn't thought about them before.

"Ylena, how is my family?" I asked her as I drove into a shopping strip across the road from the inn. We would leave the car here to be found.

"They are well," she said. "Of course, your mother was shocked when the news of your betrayal came to light. I know they endure a little prejudice for being the family of a traitor, but I checked on them often and they were well." She glanced at me. "And Adriel is sixteen now, getting ready to join the Guardians Academy."

"What?" I almost squealed. Adriel hadn't shown any signs required to join the academy. And by the light, she was sixteen already!

"She looks so much like you."

That wasn't a good thing right now. She was seen as a traitor's sister and she looked like the traitor. The academy could be a brutal place, with brutal angels, and she would suffer there.

Not if we defeated Rhodes and the truth became known.

We left the car in a random parking spot, crossed the street, and headed to the inn. We rented only one room with two beds for safety, and before we got too comfortable, Ylena suggested we train.

"This inn is in the middle of nowhere," she said. "If we walk a few yards behind it, I bet we'll find a wooded area, or an empty field."

I liked that idea.

We walked to the back of the inn, and sure enough, past the almost empty parking lot and a line of tall trees was an open field with grass up to my knees.

Ylena stopped a safe distance from the inn. "This should be a good spot."

The line of trees kept anyone at the inn from seeing us, and there was nothing except grass, and farther away, more trees around here.

I nodded and stood beside her. "I don't know the extent of my magic. Perhaps we should start with a basic spell and go from there."

She smiled at me. "It feels like old times. Though, the scenery is a little different."

I almost chuckled, even as longing filled my chest. It did feel like old times, like my first days at the academy, when we learned to summon our magic and control it little by little. Though, at the academy, the open area we train in was separated into several rings that had invisible magic barriers—in case someone lost control. This way, no one would be hurt.

Thankfully, there was no one here with us, and the inn

was several hundred yards away. Even so, I kept my back to it, so, if I lost control, I would send my magic to the trees.

"All right," Ylena started. "Take a deep breath, feel your magic, and make a light bolt in your hands."

I did as instructed. When I reached my magic, it resisted, but eventually, it gave in, and I created a bolt the size of a soccer ball in between my hands. It flickered once and I had to focus to keep its shape and power.

"Good," Ylena said, nodding.

"Not that good." I gritted my teeth. "It's fighting me."

"From what you told me, your magic has been inside dragons and dragon eggs, dormant for half a year. It's lazy and reluctant. It'll fight you."

"We don't have time for this."

"Like you said, once you push through this resistance, it'll go back to how it was before. It'll be quick." She waved her hand to the side. "Now, break it down into smaller bolts and throw them out in an arc."

"Any particular target?" Not that there was much around here.

"Not yet. Just make sure it goes a good distance."

I nodded, inhaled deeply, and focused on the big bolt between my fingers. I pulled my hands apart and imagined the bolt separating into smaller bits. Again, the magic resisted, wanting to stay together. With a grunt, I tugged harder and created six bolts from the bigger one. The magic flickered once more, but I kept a leash on it.

I pushed my hands out and sent the bolts through the air, all of them forward, but opening up and forming a big arc.

Ylena lifted her hand and closed her fist. My bolts disappeared into thin air like smoke in the night. "Good." Damn, I had forgotten how powerful she was. "Again."

I groaned. She shot me a look that said "really?" so I swallowed my frustration and did it again. This time was a bit easier. We went from the bolts, to darts, and then to bolts that became darts halfway to their target. After an hour, my arms trembled, my back had a thin sheen of sweat, and I was starting to lose my grip on my magic again.

"One more time before we take a break," Ylena said. "And this time, you can aim at these." She lifted her hands up and six figures of light appeared in the distance. "I'll keep them still for now, but later we'll try them moving. Ready?"

"No," I muttered. She gave me that look again. "Sorry."

"I know this is frustrating for a cherubin who completed her training and has been fending for herself for a while, but I wouldn't be pushing you this hard if I didn't know you could handle it. Once more, then we take a break."

"Until tomorrow?" It was past six in the evening and the sky was starting to darken. I could really use a shower, some food, and sleep.

She nodded. "Until tomorrow. Now, do it."

I took a deep breath, focused, called my magic, and formed a big bolt of light in my hands. I spliced it in six and threw them at the targets, but as I was sending them off, the little bolts flickered and two faded, turning dark.

One of the light bolts landed not ten yards from us, sizzling the tall grass. Two hit the targets and they blinked out of the existence. Another one zoomed past the target, missing it by an inch, and landed at least fifty yards behind it.

One of the darkish bolts fizzled out and disappeared

halfway to the target. The other one hit the target in the chest and—

Boom!

Bolt and target exploded in a giant light-fire. Ylena and I fell back with the blast and the ground shook.

Swiftly, Ylena jumped to her feet, moved her hands as if she was parting wind, and reined in the fire. She pulled it back, until it was the size of a tennis ball. It floated to her and landed in her open palm. She closed her hand around it and it poofed away.

Just like that.

I stared at her hand in awe.

And in frustration.

"I'm not sure I'll be ready in two or three days," I said, my tone harsher than I wanted it to be.

Ylena placed a hand on my shoulder. "You're eager to make it work, but this is the first day. The first hour. I bet that after a good night's sleep, you'll be ready for another go. Tomorrow, we can train for several hours, with breaks, and I'm sure that by the end of the day, you'll be ready. Or close to it."

I stared at her, wanting to be mad, but as usual, Ylena had this calm, serene aura around her and it was impossible to stay mad around her. She was like a mini-Adona, whose presence was an intense calming balm.

And that was why Adona was our goddess, and Ylena was the most powerful archangel in Elysium.

"I'll only believe you when it happens."

She offered me a small smile, but it turned into a frown. "Ariella, if you think about your magic and how you're training to get used to it again, to make it familiar, it isn't much different from when you first started using your magic and had to learn everything. You didn't know what you could do, how powerful you were, but you trained in a carefully controlled environment, with angels stronger than you, and you learned."

"True," I said, knowing she wasn't done.

"That's the same with the Scarlet Hex Blade." And there it was. "We can create a secure environment where we can test it and find out what it does. And once we do, we can determine if we can use it against Rhodes. If we *should* use it against him." She paused. "Imagine if we can use this weapon and win this battle without much fighting, without loss of life."

My brows curled down. "You're hoping this dagger has good power in it."

"Well, I'm always optimistic." True. "But if it doesn't, if we use it and find out it's a terrible power, we hide it and we never touch it again." Her eyes bore into mine. "I know you're worried, but this might be all we need to win."

I frowned. "You're my commanding officer, but you're acting strange. Why don't you order me to go get it?"

She shook her head. "Things have changed. We're on the run. I'm not your commanding officer right now." She offered me a tight smile. "Besides, you're a smart angel and I know you'll make the right decision for yourself."

Damn, she always knew what to say to move the needle.

With a sigh, I nodded. "All right. We can get the dagger."

"That's a smart decision. You won't regret it. Is it close?"

"Not really."

"That's okay." She turned to the inn. "Why don't we go find something to eat and discuss the details of how and when to get it over dinner?"

20

WHEN YLENA AND I CAME BACK TO OUR HOTEL ROOM, I COULD barely stand. It was like all the energy had been sucked out of me. I guess I had a big day and I hadn't stopped once. I was bound for some crash and burn.

While I took a shower, Ylena went to the shopping center across the street and bought us some burgers from a fast-food place.

I stared at her while she ate.

"What?" she asked.

"I have only seen you eating at formal dinners," I said. "Never in a million years did I think I would ever see you eating a burger."

"I'm hungry. Right now, I'll eat anything."

I knew what she meant. When I was first stuck on Earth, without money or resources, I almost starved to death. I had to fight with my moral compass to finally steal food.

Things went downhill from there.

While eating, I checked my phone. I hadn't paid attention

to it while training and now I saw a handful of calls and texts from Queen Thea.

Where are you?

You were supposed to arrive hours ago.

Ari, I'm worried. Pick up your phone.

Shit. I had been so excited about Ylena, I totally forgot about going to DuMoir Castle and meeting Zadkiel.

I sent her a text.

Sorry, I didn't mean to worry you. I had a change of plans. Thanks, though.

If she answered, I didn't see, because soon after, I went to bed. Ylena sat on her bed and turned on the TV, with the volume turned down. She said she was going to watch the news, then would sleep.

"We have a big day tomorrow," she said.

Right. The dagger. I almost shuddered at the thought of getting close to that weapon again, but I was too tired for that.

I closed my eyes.

It felt like I blinked, but when I opened my eyes again, the room was dark, except for the TV, which was still on. Ylena was half seated, half laying down on a pile of pillows, sleeping, the remote control near her hand.

I reached for my phone on the nightstand to look at the time. It was just past one in the morning. By the light, I'd slept like a rock for four hours. Maybe five.

I was about to set my phone down again and try to go back to sleep, but I saw there were several notifications.

I sat up in bed, unlocked my phone, and checked them— it was several calls and texts from Levi, and the last one had been a few minutes ago.

Frowning, I texted him.

Me: *What happened? Why aren't you sleeping?*

Levi: *Use one of your coins and open a portal.*

Me: *What is this about? Is it the bond?*

I felt it too. His absence weighed heavily inside of me, but we had been apart before. We could do it again.

Levi: *Open the fucking portal.*

Me: *Why? I'm fine, you're fine.*

I didn't want him here distracting me from my goals.

The phone vibrated with his call and I pressed the side button to stop it. The phone was silent at this time of the night, but the vibration alone could wake someone.

I went into the bathroom, closed the door, and called him.

"This better be good," I said, my voice low.

"Gwen had a vision a couple of hours ago," he said in a rush. "You need to open the portal and let me through."

I frowned. "What vision?"

"Sweetheart ..."

"Tell me!"

"She saw you being stabbed in the back, literally, and she said that would happen soon."

I processed that for a second. Then, Gwen saw me in a fight? With Rhodes? And he or someone stabbed me? And soon? That meant I would get control of my magic tomorrow, get the Scarlet Hex Blade, and go to Elysium soon!

"Levi, I appreciate the warning, but now that I know, I can watch for it, and—"

"Ariella, open the fucking portal now, or I'll leave this place right now and follow the bond, even if I have to scour Boston and the surrounding areas inch by inch."

Holy shit, the man was persistent. And of course, Abbie had told him where she had dropped me off.

Knowing he wasn't kidding, I said, "Hang on a minute."

Then I tiptoed out of the bathroom, grabbed a coin from my bag, my jacket from the armchair, and my boots from beside the door, and exited the room, careful not to make any noise when closing the door behind me.

I slipped on my shoes and my jacket, and walked to the inn's first floor, on a small path that cut below the building, where the vending machines were located. I glanced side to side, listened for a second, then I used the coin.

The moment the portal opened, Levi crossed over. Hands in fists and eyes full of murder, he looked around, making sure the danger wasn't right behind me.

"As you can see, everything is fine," I told him. "Whatever Gwen saw, it won't happen in the next two days, I think."

He finally stopped and looked at me. Even at this time of night, he was dressed in black slacks and a perfectly smooth dark blue button-up shirt that made his eyes pop—and right now they looked like two fiery stones.

"It won't happen in two days," he said, his tone low, harsh.

"What?"

"What Gwen saw, she said it was soon. As in, a few hours."

"Unless another group of supernaturals finds us again, or angels, then I don't think we'll encounter anyone to harm us."

"Us?"

"Yeah." I smiled at him. "My mentor found me earlier today." Then I remembered it was after midnight. "Or yesterday. Whatever."

"Your mentor?"

"Yeah, I told you about her. She's the most powerful archangel in Elysium. Her name is—"

"Ylena." His eyes shifted to a point above my shoulder.

When I turned, Ylena stood a dozen feet or so behind me, near the path's entrance.

Then I realized he had said her name. "You know her?"

"Hi, Leviathan," Ylena said.

My brows curled down. "You know each other?"

Levi slipped his big hand into mine and tugged me closer to him. He pointed a finger to Ylena. "Stay back." Then he took a couple of steps back, taking me with him. "Do not move."

"Levi, that's my mentor." I tried taking my hand from his, to stop moving back, but his grip only tightened. "What are you doing? Stop this."

"It has been so long, Leviathan," Ylena said, her tone almost eerie. "I heard you were helping Ariella."

I snapped my head to her. "What?"

Levi turned to me and grabbed my shoulders. "Remember I wanted to tell you something a couple of days ago?"

I nodded, confused. "What does that have to do with this?"

"Everything!" he almost shouted. "Fuck it. You'll hate me again anyway. Ariella, Ylena is—"

"I'm his mother," Ylena said.

I blinked, I shook my head, I almost fell back. What? That didn't make sense. Ylena was an archangel and she was thousands of years old. She went through the academy when she was young, and she had become sterile then ...

But Levi was twenty-eight.

I took a step back. "It can't be."

"I know what you're thinking," Ylena said. "That I can't have children. It turns out, I can. I am the only angel who went through the academy who still can." She took a couple of steps closer.

Levi retreated, taking me with him. I was too numb to protest. "Stay back!"

"You see," she went on, ignoring him. "I created that rule over a thousand years ago when I had my first child. He had become one of the most powerful angels I had ever seen. One day, we went on a mission together, but we underestimated our enemies. I got distracted, trying to protect him, and let our enemy win. Adona almost stripped me of my rank. Not long after, he died in battle while I was benched."

"So, you proposed the sterilization process," I muttered.

She nodded. "Adona and the other archangels thought it was a marvelous idea."

"But you didn't go through the process."

"I should have, but I think I was too distraught. I felt like ... if I went through the process, then it was like I never had my son." She swallowed hard. "That was when my hatred for Adona gained roots."

My jaw slacked. "What?"

"You're the one behind it all, not Rhodes," Levi said, sounding as stunned as I was.

"I shouldn't feel pride for your intelligence, alas ..." She shrugged.

Levi snarled. "You don't feel anything, bitch. If you did, you wouldn't abandon a baby minutes after he was born."

"When you were in my stomach, I could feel you were ninety-nine percent demon and almost nothing angel," she barked back. "I wanted nothing to do with you."

Levi tried to hide it, but he flinched. "How about not sleeping with a demon in the first place?"

"As if you haven't slept with the wrong person before."

I stared at them, trying to process what they were saying, what was happening here, and I felt like I was drowning in molasses.

It was Ylena who started all of this. She was the one who wanted to take over Elysium. She had recruited Rhodes and the others.

And to top it all, she had slept with the enemy and had his child.

Levi knew Ylena was his mother, but he hadn't known she was the one who had—

I gasped. "You sent me on that mission to die!"

"I didn't!" Ylena shouted. "I had sent Cyan, but he couldn't go so you volunteered! I told Soren that you weren't qualified enough to go, a lie, to get you out of it, but Soren thought you were amazing, so he took you. Before you left, I was already mourning you."

I took a large step back, my chest heaving, my heart hurting.

"You're the one who wanted the dagger." I pressed a hand to my chest. "And now you are tricking me. Pretending to be at odds with Rhodes so I would take you to the dagger!"

"Smart and pretty," Ylena said, not amused.

"What does that dagger do exactly?" I asked. If she wanted it so bad, she knew.

"As if I would tell you." She scoffed. "Just know it's enough to kill Adona." She looked at Levi. "And any other supernatural. Isn't that right?"

I looked at Levi. "You wanted the dagger."

He pointed at Ylena. "To kill her."

But he didn't know about her rebellion. He wanted to kill her for leaving him and not looking back.

A little extreme, but Levi was extreme.

"Listen, Ariella, I never wanted to kill you," Ylena said. "I never wanted to hunt you and put a reward on your head, but when you ran with the dagger, you gave me no choice." She extended her hand to me. "Come with me now. Let me show you why we need to eliminate Adona and all these old, ridiculous rules, and start our society anew. I know you'll understand, and once you do, you'll join me."

I stared at her, appalled. "Even if Adona is wrong and the rules should be changed, killing her and her supporters isn't the answer."

"That's how every revolution starts!"

I took a step back. "I'll never go with you, and I'll never give you the dagger."

She growled, light magic enveloping her hands. "I almost had her. I almost had the dagger, but you had to show up and mess with everything." She threw a light bolt at Levi.

He was quick and deflected it with a darkfire bolt. "Let us go," he said. "Let us go and I won't kill you."

Ylena laughed. "You can't kill me!" She threw a huge light bolt at us.

Levi lifted his arm, creating a thin wall of shadows, as he reached for my hand and grabbed it. He turned to the portal, but the shadows parted and Ylena sent her magic toward the portal. It started small, like a tennis ball, but it grew as it got to the portal, and stretched like a net, swallowing the portal. It returned to ball size and then sizzled away in the air.

"Fuck," Levi muttered. Holding my hand tight, he sent a

cascade of darkfire darts toward Ylena—his freaking mother!—and ran with me toward the back of the inn.

"Wait," I said, unsure we should wait. I felt like hitting pause on all of this. I needed time to think, to process.

"We don't have time," Levi said, squeezing my hand. "Just ... let's get out of here. We can talk, argue, or whatever once we're safe."

Safe. From Ylena. The angel I had looked up to my entire life.

Levi's mother.

I should be mad at him for this, for not telling me sooner, but this time, it was on me. I was the one who didn't want to talk about our lives—even though he knew almost everything about mine.

We ran to the field where Ylena and I trained earlier. "Do you know where we're going?"

"No. The plan is to run until we can hide, or until we find a car."

There were cars at the front of the inn, but if we stopped and turned now, we would come face-to-face with Ylena.

"You don't have another coin, do you?"

I shook my head.

We were halfway through the field when the targets made of light appeared before us, but this time, it wasn't six. It was at least fifteen and they moved, with weapons made of light, closing in around us.

Levi suddenly stopped and pulled me closer to him.

"You have nowhere to run," Ylena said as she joined the line of her light soldiers. "And you can't possibly win against me. Just surrender."

She was right. We couldn't win a direct fight against her. But there had to be another way.

"And then what?" I asked, trying to gain some time while thinking how we could escape her.

"And then I promise to take you in and put you in a good house in Elysium with your family, after you tell me where to find the dagger."

"So like a prison."

"A comfortable prison."

"What about him?" I asked, pointing my chin at Levi. I couldn't read his thoughts, but I knew that like me, he was running several scenarios in his mind to find a way for us to get out of this one without any fatal wounds.

She stared at Levi. "I promise to let him go, as long as he doesn't interfere in any of this anymore."

"I can't do that," he said through gritted teeth.

"Aw, because of an accidental bond you two share?" she teased. I suppressed a gasp. "I know almost everything, Ariella, don't be so surprised."

"It might have been accidental, but it's real," Levi said. My eyes became two huge balls. He shifted his gaze to me. "I won't let anyone break it."

My heart stopped for what felt like an entire minute, before kicking it into high gear.

"Foolish demon, stupid angel," she hissed. A huge bolt of light formed in her hands and all of her light soldiers pointed their weapons at us. "Last chance. Surrender."

Levi continued looking at me. "Sweetheart, wish for me to take her to the fiery pits of the underworld."

Oh, I liked that idea. "I wish you to take her to the fiery pits of the underworld."

He offered me that lopsided grin that was starting to grow on me, brought my hand to his lips, kissed the top of my hand, his lips warm and soft.

Then, he let go of me and ran toward Ylena.

Taking her by surprise, he threw a darkfire at her, making her lose the grip on her bolt, and lunged at her.

The moment his arms closed around her, both of them disappeared.

Even the light soldiers faded like sparkly smoke.

I stared at the spot where they had been a second ago, despair clawing at my chest.

What had I done?

ENJOYING ARIELLA'S AND LEVI'S STORY? THEN DON'T MISS book 3, Fallen Demons: https://julianahaygertbooks.com/products/fallen-demon

Join my Facebook group (https://www.facebook.com/groups/JulianasClub) to get another exclusive book, *The Light Witch*.

Last but not least, you can check out the recommended reading order here: https://www.julianahaygert.com/wp-content/uploads/2024/02/Rite-World-Reading-Order.pdf You can download, print, and check the books you've already read! Enjoy!

THANK YOU

THANK YOU FOR READING *LIGHT MAGIC*!

Reviews are very important for authors. If you liked my book, please consider leaving a review on my store, your favorite online retailer and/or on Goodreads and/or Bookbub, please!

DID YOU LIKE THIS BOOK? YOU CAN CHECK OUT OTHER BOOKS of mine:

The Night Calling (Rite World: Night Wolves book 1): she was abandoned by her mate, left in the hands of a terrible half-demon ... but now he's back and ready to claim her.

The Darkest Vampire (Rite World: Vampire Wars book 1): a witch releases a dark vampire from a curse, and becomes inadvertently bonded to him.

The Midnight Test (Rite World: Lightgrove Witches book 1): a clueless witch is invited to join a powerful coven—but only if she aces a difficult test.

The Demon Kiss (Rite World: Blackthorn Hunters

Academy book 1): a fast-paced story about a young woman who finds out she's a demon hunter, and the half-demon intent on protecting her against all evil.

The Vampire Heir (Rite World 1: Rite of the Vampire): a dark and mysterious paranormal romance about a vampire and a young woman with a secret.

The Warlock Lord (Rite World 4: Rite of the Warlock): a thrilling and kick-ass paranormal romance about a werewolf and warlock.

The Wolf Forsaken (Rite World 7: Rite of the Wolf): a heat-wrenching tale about a lost wolf shifter and a fae princess on the run.

Winter King (The Wyth Courts book 1): a fae king needs to sacrifice a pure-hearted human to save his kingdom from a terrible curse. Only, he soon finds out she's his fated mate.

Heart Seeker (The Fire Heart Chronicles book 1): an urban fantasy series about a young woman who finds herself at the center of a mysterious supernatural world.

Destiny Gift (The Everlast Series book 1): a post-apocalyptic urban fantasy series about a young woman with a special power that can save the world.

IF YOU WANT TO SEE EXCLUSIVE TEASERS, HELP ME DECIDE ON covers, read excerpts, talk about books, etc, join my reader group on Facebook: Juliana's Club!

ABOUT THE AUTHOR

While USA Today Bestselling Author Juliana Haygert dreams of being Wonder Woman, Buffy, or a blood elf shadow priest, she settles for the less exciting—but equally gratifying—life as a wife, a mother, and an author. She resides in North Carolina and spends her days writing about kick-ass heroines and the heroes who drive them crazy.

For more information:
www.julianahaygert.com

facebook.com/julianahaygert

x.com/julianahaygert

instagram.com/juliana.haygert

goodreads.com/juliana_haygert

pinterest.com/julianahaygert

bookbub.com/authors/juliana-haygert

youtube.com/julianahaygert

tiktok.com/@julianahaygert

ALSO BY JULIANA HAYGERT

To find links and more info, go to:
www.julianahaygertbooks.com

Standalones
Daughter of Darkness

Rite World: Fallen Angel
Dark Wings (Book 1)
Light Magic (Book 2)
Fallen Demon (Book 3)
Wicked Angel (Book 4)

Rite World: Night Wolves
The Night Calling (Book 1)
The Night Burning (Book 2)
The Night Hunting (Book 3)
The Night Rising (Book 4)

Rite World: Vampire Wars
The Darkest Vampire (Book 1)
The Darkest Witch (Book 2)
The Darkest Magic (Book 3)

Rite World: Lightgrove Witches
The Midnight Test (Book 1)
The Midnight Spell (Book 2)
The Midnight Flame (Book 3)
The Midnight Secret (Book 4)
The Midnight Hunt (Book 5)
The Midnight Wish (Book 6)

Rite World: Blackthorn Hunters Academy

The Demon Kiss (Book 1)
The Hunter Secret (Book 2)
The Soul Bond (Book 3)
The Shadow Trials (Book 4)
The Infernal Curse (Book 5)

Rite World

The Vampire Heir (Book 1)
The Witch Queen (Book 2)
The Immortal Vow (Book 3)
The Warlock Lord (Book 4)
The Wolf Consort (Book 5)
The Crystal Rose (Book 6)
The Wolf Forsaken (Book 7)
The Fae Bound (Book 8)
The Blood Pact (Book 9)

The Wyth Courts

Winter King (Book 1)
Spring Warrior (Book 2)
Summer Prince (Book 3)
Autumn Rebel (Book 4)

The Fire Heart Chronicles

Heart Seeker (Book 1)
Flame Caster (Book 2)
Earth Shaker (Book 2.5)
Sorrow Bringer (Book 3)
Soul Wanderer (Book 4)
Fate Summoner (Book 5)
War Maiden (Book 6)

The Everlast Series

Destiny Gift (Book 1)
Soul Oath (Book 2)
Cup of Life (Book 3)
Everlasting Circle (Book 4)

<u>*Willow Harbor Series*</u>
Hunter's Revenge (Book 3)
Siren's Song (Book 5)

<u>*Breaking Series*</u>
Breaking Free (Book 1)
Breaking Away (Book 2)
Breaking Through (Book 3)
Breaking Down (Book 4)